"Johnny, how long have we been married?"

He hesitated only a moment. "It seems like only yesterday, kitten."

Marla frowned. Was he being intentionally evasive? Or didn't their wedding date mean anything to him? Twisting her ring, she closed her eyes and tried to picture herself in a wedding gown. An image actually formed—a long gown with a low-cut bodice, a strand of pearls and a veil hiding the bride's face. She searched her memory for a picture of the groom, of Johnny in a dark tux looking so handsome he'd take her breath away.

She sighed and opened her eyes when the memory failed to materialize. "I wish I could remember the details, but the harder I try—"

"The doctor said to let the memories come naturally and not to force yourself."

Gritting her teeth, she thought, *To hell with the doctor!* "You sure you wouldn't like to share the details of our honeymoon? That's something a woman really ought to remember."

His dark-eyed gaze swept over her slowly, sensuously lingering on her breasts and the fullness of her belly. "I'll tell you this, kitten. You were the greatest, absolutely the greatest...."

ABOUT THE AUTHOR

Charlotte Maclay can't resist a happy ending. That's why she's had such fun writing more than twenty titles for Harlequin American Romance and Love & Laughter, plus several Silhouette Romance books as well. Particularly well-known for her volunteer efforts in her hometown of Torrance, California, Charlotte's philosophy is that you should make a difference in your community. She and her husband have two married daughters and two grandchildren, whom they are occasionally allowed to baby-sit. She loves to hear from readers and can be reached at: P.O. Box 505, Torrance, CA 9508.

Books by Charlotte Maclay

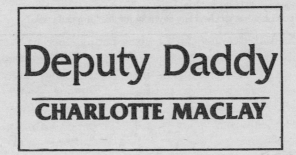

Deputy Daddy

CHARLOTTE MACLAY

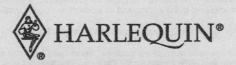

TORONTO • NEW YORK • LONDON
AMSTERDAM • PARIS • SYDNEY • HAMBURG
STOCKHOLM • ATHENS • TOKYO • MILAN • MADRID
PRAGUE • WARSAW • BUDAPEST • AUCKLAND

ISBN 0-373-16788-1

DEPUTY DADDY

This edition published by arrangement with Harlequin Books S.A.

Visit us at www.romance.net

Printed in U.S.A.

Special thanks to Anna Munro and Dan Patterson at The Soldier Factory in Cambria, California, for their warm welcome and detailed information. Your exquisite miniatures inspired me.

Prologue

A scream rose in her throat as a stake-bed truck barreled out of the fog heading straight for her on the hairpin turn. He was traveling too fast for the narrow highway that twisted and turned above the rocky coastline of central California, a few miles north of Mar del Oro.

Jerking the steering wheel, she tried to hug the right shoulder of the road with her Mercedes, but the truck was too far over the center line. A battered guardrail stood as mute testimony to how many vehicles had barely escaped disaster on these cliffs. Thirty feet below, waves buffeted the shore at high tide, spraying mist and salt into the air.

She shouldn't have tried to drive this route after dark. She'd been late....

Grimly, she steered ever closer to the railing.

The driver of the truck was bearing down on her as though he owned the entire highway. Her foot reached for the brake pedal.

She gasped as the truck slipped past her car with mere inches to spare. She hardly had time to draw a second breath when she felt metal connect with metal, heard the shrieking.

Tires squealed.

The rear end of the Mercedes lost its grip on the roadway. The car fishtailed. Ahead of her a gap in the guardrail loomed, the fog and ocean an indistinguishable misty gray beyond the opening.

Frantically, she tried to remember what to do in a skid. She twisted the wheel in what she hoped was the right direction and pumped the brakes. But it was too little, too late. She was already airborne. Weightless, the seat belt pulled hard against her distended abdomen.

Instinctively, as though she could protect her unborn baby, her hand covered her stomach, and she turned sideways away from the steering wheel.

"Dear God! Please don't let my baby die." Tears of determination blurred her vision. She wouldn't give in to the terror that filled her chest. Not now. Not after she had survived the worst life had to offer.

The car nosed over in a steep dive toward a sea of gray. The scream that had been lodged in her throat ripped free.

A moment later, everything went black.

Chapter One

"Hi, Tina." With a smile and a wink at the waitress, Johnny Fuentes sauntered to the back of the café and took a seat at his usual booth where he could keep an eye on the tourist traffic cruising the main street of Mar del Oro. He adjusted the police special he wore holstered at his hip, a concession to his job as the chief of the small police force in town.

Tina arrived within moments with a pot of coffee, a mug and a welcoming smile.

"Hi, hon," she said, pouring the coffee. She had dark, sparkling eyes and a smile so wide it was impossible not to grin back at her. "I've still got some banana cream pie if you want a slice. Or do you want something more?"

"Pie sounds good. I could use a little pick-me-up."

"The bad guys gettin' to you these days?"

"Not the bad guys. It's the mayor who's the real pain in the…" He shrugged, catching himself before he said too much. The mayor and city council might be giving him a hard time about his budget request, but he did owe them his job. It was the paperwork that was killing him. He'd spent hours at the computer and his eyes felt like they were permanently crossed. "How's it going with you?"

"Same tired feet." Glancing around to check that no other late-evening customers needed her at the moment, Tina slid into the booth opposite him. She'd dyed her hair henna red a couple of years ago and wore it cut short for comfort. "I'm off in a half hour. You want to try Hanratty's for a nightcap?"

"Sure. I'll have to stop by the house to change clothes first. Wouldn't want to give del Oro's finest a bad reputation."

She gave him a sly smile. "We could always have the nightcap at your place."

"Watch it, sweetheart." He chuckled. "Now you're really going to ruin my reputation."

"Anytime you're willing, *I* certainly am." She pursed her full lips in a mock kiss, then slid out of the booth. "Be right back with your pie."

Johnny watched her walk away, appreciating the feminine sway of her hips. Ever since he'd come back to Mar del Oro to take the chief's job, his mother had been badgering him to get serious about a girl. Any girl. *Settle down,* she kept admonishing him. *Raise me some grandbabies.*

Johnny wouldn't mind doing that. He enjoyed women as much or more than the next guy. Eventually, he'd like to have a family. But he had yet to click with one particular woman. Given the couple of dates he'd had with Tina, he didn't think she'd be the one.

To Mama's dismay, he supposed. *And* Tina's, he suspected. She had the look of a woman ready to tie the knot with any guy who wore pants. And he didn't mean that thought unkindly.

Johnny simply wasn't in that much of a hurry to get married just so his mother could have more grandchildren living nearby. Since two of his sisters had moved away, taking their children with them, Mama Fuentes was looking for a way to fill up the hole in her life.

The pager at his waist vibrated, and he looked down to check the number. The dispatcher at the station wanted him.

He levered himself out of the booth. "Okay to use your phone, Tina?" She waved her permission, and he punched in dispatch's number. "Fuentes here."

"Sorry to bother you, Chief, but we've got a report of a woman walking on the beach."

He smiled. "Patty, people walk on our beaches all the time. Particularly the tourists. That's why they come here."

"This sounds different, sir. I mean, the guy who called it in said she was acting funny."

Tourists had an odd habit of doing that, too, but Johnny didn't bother to mention that to Patty. She'd been around police work long enough to have pretty good instincts about what was right and what wasn't. "Where is she?"

"North of town about ten miles, just south of Creek Canyon. I tried to pass it on to the highway patrol, but their nearest car is handling an accident way north at Big Sur. They thought it'd be an hour or more before they could respond."

"Okay, I'll take it." Likely a tourist high on something, or a local girl who'd decided to walk home from her date. Checking it out shouldn't take long.

Hanging up the phone, he pulled his wallet out and placed a couple of dollars on the counter.

"Going to have to take a rain check on that pie, Tina."

Her broad smile dissolved. "That's too bad. How 'bout Hanratty's?"

"I'll have to see." He checked his watch. It was almost nine o'clock, the time Tina got off work. "You want to take a chance and meet me there? Or should I give you a call if I can make it?"

"Honey, I'll meet you any time, any place."

He smiled, amused at her eagerness. Troubled, too. If their relationship wasn't going anywhere, he didn't want to lead her on. He didn't want to hurt her feelings, either. This dating game was a tough business with lots of potholes in the road.

Maybe Mama was right. At thirty-one he ought to be settling down.

CONTRARY TO WHAT most people expected, summer was the foggiest time of the year along the coast. As the inland valleys heated up, marine air was pulled into the coastal regions. Tonight it hung as thick as cotton balls along the shoreline, drifting in misty clouds over the highway.

Fortunately, there wasn't much traffic. Cruising

slowly, Johnny could keep his attention half on the road and half searching the rocky beach. He wasn't very optimistic about finding anyone. By now, the wandering woman could have returned to her own car or been picked up by someone. He sure hadn't spotted any vehicles parked along the narrow shoulder.

He'd about reached the limit of his search area when he pulled over and got out of the car. The yellow lights on the top of his cruiser barely cut through the gloom. The headlights bounced back off the fog as if a mirror had been placed in the road. In the distance, invisible waves rolled against the shoreline, their sound muted by the heavy air.

As he stood peering into the fog toward the beach, the cloud lifted.

There she was! Acting funny.

At the edge of the water, she was carefully placing one foot in front of the other as if she was some kind of robot. In spite of the chill air, she was wearing a summer dress that clung damply to her legs. A small, decorative scarf was tied around her neck and her hair hung lankly to her shoulders. Definitely a woman in trouble.

He dashed across the road, climbed over the guardrail and scrambled down the cliff to the beach.

"Hey, lady! Do you need help?"

She kept on walking.

He caught up with her but didn't touch her. He didn't know what was wrong and didn't want her to freak out. "Ma'am, I'm Johnny Fuentes, chief of the Mar del Oro police. Can I help you, ma'am?"

She didn't stop.

"Ma'am, what's your name? Maybe I can help you."

Slowing, she turned toward him, her eyes as glazed as slate polished by the sea. A lump the size of a baseball disfigured her forehead and blood caked her hairline.

He swallowed a silent curse. God only knew how she'd gotten into this fix. Chances were good he wouldn't be seeing Tina any time soon tonight.

He took another look at her and suddenly realized she must be about nine months pregnant. Not wanting to frighten her, he gently took her arm.

Her mouth moved. "Wh—"

"Mar del Oro, ma'am. You're safe now." He guided her toward the road. She didn't appear to be very old. Less than thirty, he'd guess. Probably five foot six, and except for the pregnancy, would have weighed maybe a hundred and ten pounds max. Slender bones. Oval face, even features. Blond hair matted as though she'd been for a swim. "Can you tell me your name or what happened to you?"

She shook her head. "Mar...la."

"Your name's Mar? Mar what?"

Her eyes rolled up until only the whites showed. With a sigh, she simply crumpled, her legs giving out from beneath her.

Johnny caught her before she hit the ground. "Come on, Mara or Marla, whoever you are. Don't give out on me now." He lifted her in his arms, struggled with her up the steep bank to the road, then carried her to the car, placing her in the back seat.

As soon as he got the cruiser moving, he radioed headquarters and asked Patty to warn Mar del Oro Hospital he was bringing a patient into Emergency. His ETA was fifteen minutes. He hoped that would be soon enough to save the woman curled up in the back seat. And her baby.

As he drove along the highway, he watched for any sign there'd been an accident. He didn't see a thing. Tomorrow when the fog lifted, he'd have to have the area checked again.

He couldn't help but wonder who the woman in his cruiser might be. And where her husband was tonight. The splashy ring on her finger suggested he had megabucks. So did the tasteful gold earrings.

Way out of the league of a small-town police chief.

AFTER LETTING TINA KNOW he'd be tied up for several hours, Johnny waited at the hospital, hoping the woman would come to. If she'd been in an accident, someone else might have been involved—a passenger or another vehicle. Or she might be a victim of foul play. Either way, he'd have to investigate.

He idled away his time chatting with the night admissions clerk, a cute little gal from San Luis Obispo, a fair-size college town about forty minutes away. He promised her he'd go to the farmers' market there one of these days.

Dr. Bernie, a long, lanky runner wearing eyeglasses a half-inch thick, appeared in the lobby.

With a smile and a "See you" to the clerk, Johnny shoved himself away from the reception counter. "How is she, Doc?"

"She's got a fairly serious concussion and multiple bruises and contusions. We won't know for sure about her condition for twenty-four hours. For the moment, she's stable."

"How 'bout the baby?"

"Good heartbeat. Very active." He slipped his hands into the pockets of his white jacket. "It's a girl, by the way. Due in about a month, we're guessing."

The tension that had been plaguing the back of Johnny's neck eased now that he knew the woman and her baby were in reasonably good shape. "Can I talk with her?"

"You can try. She's been in and out of consciousness, a little disoriented. Which is understandable. She took quite a wallop on her head. I've given her a mild sedative so she can rest." He turned to lead Johnny back through the double doors to the patients' wing. "Did she tell you her name?"

"She tried to. Mar something. Marla, maybe?"

"How about next of kin?"

"She didn't have any ID on her. I'm hoping she can tell me what happened." Most of the patient rooms were dark. From one of them came a soft moaning, as though the occupant was in pain. The nurse on duty gave them a wave as they passed the nurses' station. "Do you have any idea what caused her injuries?"

"From the bruising across her chest and abdomen,

I'd say a car accident. It looks like a seat belt did the damage—and probably saved her life and the baby's, too.''

But where was the car? Johnny wondered. And had there been other passengers?

The fixture over the bed cast a dim light toward the ceiling, softening the room with shadows. They'd hooked her up to an IV, and a bandage now covered the injuries on her forehead. Something tightened in Johnny's chest at seeing her look so pale and vulnerable. He'd always been a sucker for anyone who was sick or hurt. That's probably why he'd become a cop—not to catch the crooks so much as to help those they'd injured.

He leaned over the bed. ''Ma'am, can you hear me? Is there someone I can call for you? Your husband? Marla, can you hear me?''

Her eyelids fluttered.

''Can you tell me where your husband is?'' And if he'd been in the car with her.

She licked her lips. Her eyes opened. In this light, the slate-gray he'd noted before was now sea-green. Ever so slowly, a smile curled her lips. ''I knew you'd come,'' she whispered. Her eyes closed, but the smile didn't leave her lips.

Johnny frowned, then glanced at the doctor. ''What do you make of that?''

''It's the concussion.'' He shrugged. ''Confusion is to be expected. She'll do better tomorrow, I imagine.''

But meanwhile, where was her car? And her husband?

SHE MOVED AND A VISE tightened around her chest. That set up another round of sledgehammers inside her skull. She moaned. What was the matter with her? What awful dream—

"You can wake up now. Take it easy. Just open your eyes, Marla. Very slowly."

Someone was talking, but she wasn't sure they were talking to her. A man's voice. Pleasant but not familiar. She tried to ignore him in the hope the sledgehammers would stop pounding.

"That's it. Easy now. You're doing fine. And so is your baby."

Her eyes flew open. A serious mistake. Pain seared through her head, through her whole body. She caught only a quick glimpse of a man standing over her before she closed her eyes again. Her arm felt weighted as she dragged it up and palmed her abdomen. *Her baby.* She was all right.

Relief sent her toward the black pit where she hadn't felt any pain.

"Don't go back to sleep, Marla. We need to talk."

My, but he was a determined man. Why wouldn't he let her sleep?

"I'm Dr. Bernie. You're in a hospital in Mar del Oro."

Hospital? She tried to frown, but it hurt too much. Was she having her baby already? It was too soon,

wasn't it? This isn't how they said labor would feel—
like a bone crusher had a hold of her head.

"Can you tell me your name?"

Silly man. He'd just called her Marla and he ought
to know. He'd said he was her doctor. Carefully, she
rolled the name through her mind, seeing if it fit. She
thought it did, so she was certainly willing to take the
doctor's word for it.

"Do you know who the president of the United
States is?"

Good grief! Now he was giving her an IQ test.
What she needed was a whole bottle of aspirin. Why
did the doctor want to confuse her with a bunch of
ridiculous questions? Of course she knew who the
president was. But with the headache she had, she
didn't much care.

"We want to notify your husband that you've been
in an accident. Can you tell us where to reach him?"

An image swam through the haze of pain like a red
tide. Her husband? She tried to picture him, to anchor
her confused thoughts in a semblance of reality. The
image formed, then slid apart like a broken jigsaw
puzzle and came together again. Dark hair, a slightly
crooked smile and sympathetic eyes. Yes, he'd be the
one. *Someone who could love her.*

"He knows where I am," she whispered. Her
throat was rough and raspy, like sandpaper; her mouth
was as dry as toast. "He was here." She'd seen him.
Johnny. She remembered him saying his name was
Johnny.

"Your husband was here?"

She nodded, another serious mistake. The pounding inside her head nearly drowned out the doctor's question. "You met him. He has…simpatico eyes."

Determined to ignore the doctor, she carried the image of those sympathetic eyes back into her private world of darkness where there was no more pain, no more bleak disappointment or betrayal. Only hope, understanding and love.

FIRST THING IN THE MORNING, Johnny sent two squad cars to patrol the length of Highway 1 from Big Sur south to Morro Bay. They didn't see any sign of a recent accident. No abandoned cars. No newly damaged guardrail. No one searching the beach for a missing wife or loved one.

When he checked the notices from other law enforcement agencies, he found no report of a missing person matching Marla's description.

So far it seemed she'd appeared out of the sea all on her own. With a name like Marla, that made a certain amount of warped sense, assuming you spoke a little Spanish.

He grinned at the thought as he pulled into the hospital parking lot. His own personal sea nymph. That ought to make Mama happy.

Inside the hospital, he made his way down the hallway toward the woman's room. Bustling nurses, aides and orderlies had replaced the quiet of the night before, and periodically the loudspeaker paged maintenance or a doctor.

Dr. Bernie caught him at the nurses' station. "Before you see our patient, there's something you need to know.''

The doctor's tone warned Johnny something was wrong. To expect another victim, maybe. ''What's up?''

''She appears to be suffering from amnesia. That's not terribly unusual with head injuries and it typically subsides after the swelling around the brain goes down.''

''So she doesn't know who she is or what happened to her?''

''That's right. I had to tell her the baby is a girl. But there's another little twist to the story that's going to affect you more directly than a simple case of amnesia.'' He took off his glasses and polished them with the handkerchief he'd pulled from his jacket pocket.

''Don't hold back, Doc. It looks like I've got a mystery on my hands. Anything you can tell me about her will help.''

Dr. Bernie slipped the glasses back on and adjusted the wire rims over his ears. ''The young woman you brought in last night is convinced that you are her husband...and the father of her unborn child.''

Chapter Two

"You're kidding." Johnny stared at Dr. Bernie as though the doctor had announced he'd acquired a second head. "I never saw her before last night."

"She certainly described you to a T." The doctor grinned. "Including your simpatico eyes that every girl in town is crazy about."

Johnny had the good grace to blush. Could he help it if women liked him and he reciprocated the feeling? "I hope you told the lady she was wrong about me."

"Every time I tried to pursue that line of conversation, she became very agitated. Alarmingly so, given her delicate condition."

"You can't let her go on believing—"

"I see no harm in it at the moment. And it's probably safer for now to let her believe what she wants to. She's been severely traumatized by whatever happened to her and is probably subconsciously trying to repress some unpleasant memories. Since it seems to give her some comfort to think of you as her husband, I see no difficulty."

"The difficulty is she's got a husband someplace who's got to be looking for her."

"Fine. When he shows up, I'm reasonably confident he will jog her memory back to where it belongs. The amnesia is only a temporary condition, at any rate."

"How temporary?" Johnny wanted to know.

"We could walk in her room right now and she might know you aren't her husband."

"Great."

"Or it could be a week or a month from now." He picked up a chart from the stand at the end of the counter and flipped it open. "More than ninety percent of all amnesia victims fully recover their memories."

"What about the other ten percent?"

The doctor gave the question some thought. "Why don't we take an optimistic view for the moment? Give it a day or two to sort itself out. I need to observe her for at least another twenty-four hours."

Carrying the chart, the doctor headed down the corridor away from Marla's room. Johnny followed him.

"Wait a minute, Doc. Are you saying I'm supposed to pretend to be this woman's husband until she decides otherwise?"

"No, not at all. My suggestion would be not to make an issue of it. The calmer we can keep her, the more rapid her recovery should be. Given her condition, I don't want to cause her so much upset that we get an early onset of labor. Excessive distress wouldn't be healthy for either mother or baby."

Well, hell! Johnny didn't want to cause her any distress, but she already had a husband who should be here with her. Johnny didn't have the vaguest idea of how to find him, however. Not until someone came through with a missing-person report. And if she'd been traveling somewhere alone, that could take days.

Meanwhile, he was supposed to play the part of devoted husband?

Man alive, he didn't want to deceive any woman like that. What would she think when she came back to her senses? For that matter, what would everybody else in town think if they got wind of this charade?

Still, he couldn't leave the poor woman alone in her room wondering where on earth her husband was and why he hadn't come to claim her. Not when she'd been hurt so badly. That kind of worry wouldn't be good for her kid, either.

Temporary.

The doc had said her memory might come back any minute. Johnny didn't suppose a little deception would hurt if it was in the best interests of the patient—two of them in this case. And as police chief, he had sworn to protect and serve the residents of Mar del Oro. Marla whatever-her-name was the newest inhabitant of his fair city.

He owed her his best.

THE BLINDS IN THE ROOM had been tilted to let in the morning sunlight, striping the bed with light and shadow. Her color was better today in spite of the absence of makeup, and someone had made an effort to brush her hair. But the bandage on her forehead was an ugly reminder of the accident she'd suffered, along with the shiner that had developed on her left eye.

Sensing his presence, the woman opened her eyes. Johnny held his breath. Maybe she'd recognize him as the stranger he was.

Her gentle smile reached her eyes, expressing both relief and recognition. ''Hi.''

"Hi yourself. You're looking better today."

"I've still got an anvil chorus going on in my head." She reached out her hand to him.

Under the circumstances, Johnny could hardly refuse her invitation. He crossed the room to her bedside and closed his big hand around hers.

She winced.

"What's wrong?"

"I must have fallen on my hands. They're both scraped."

He turned her hand over to examine her palm. From the redness and scratches, he'd guess she'd been doing some impromptu rock climbing without gloves. She must have been out there in the dark and fog for a long time. No woman—particularly one who was pregnant—should have had to go through that ordeal alone.

Worse, given her injuries, it was going to be hard to get a good set of fingerprints until her hands healed.

When he looked up, he found her studying his uniform, the badge on his chest and the weapon he carried. "I feel so silly. I didn't even remember you're a policeman."

"I'm the chief, actually."

"There, you see? They've poked and prodded me until I can't even remember what my own husband does for a living." Her chin quivered, and she squeezed his hand more tightly, her slender fingers in a death grip. "I feel so lost."

A rush of sympathy welled in Johnny's chest. Despite her injuries, he liked the feel of her hand, the look of her fair complexion against his darker one, and he had to forcefully remind himself that this woman wasn't available. "The doctor says you'll be fine. You just have to give yourself a little time."

"I can't even remember how I got here. What happened to me, Johnny?"

"We think it was a car accident."

"I think I remember you finding me, rescuing me on the beach. My blue knight."

He'd been called a lot of things but never a knight, presumably one in shining armor. That was a heavy responsibility. "You were pretty well out of it by the time I got you to the hospital."

"Thank goodness the baby wasn't hurt." With her free hand, the one with the diamond wedding ring, she covered her belly. "She keeps letting me know she's still in there and ready to go. From the feel of it, I think she's going to be an Olympic gymnast."

The pride in her voice and the love he heard made Johnny smile. Even if she didn't know who she was or where she was from, she was going to be a good mother.

"She'll be the greatest, I'm sure," he said.

"I can't remember. Were you a gymnast in high school?"

"I was more into football. Played quarterback."

"I should know that, shouldn't I?" She struggled, trying to scoot up a little higher in the bed. "I can't understand why everything is such a blank—"

"Shh, you'll be all right. And it's not good for you or the baby if you get too upset. You need your rest now."

"I know. That's what the doctor said. But I wish I could go home."

Johnny wished he knew where her home was. "Yeah, but not just yet. You take a nap and I'll drop by later to check on you."

"All right." She finally released her grip on his hand. "And Johnny, when you come back, could you bring me some makeup?"

"Uh, sure. What kind do you want?"

Her forehead pleated as though she was trying to remember the answer to that question. "Whatever's on the bathroom counter will do."

"Great. I'll, uh, do that." He backed toward the door.

"And would you bring me my nightgown, too? The rear view of this hospital gown is downright obscene."

His lips twitched. "I guess it would be." He imagined if the situation were different, he'd find it an attractive view. "I'll see what I can find for you."

"Thank you," she whispered as he retreated into the hallway.

Well, hell! Once out of sight, he leaned back against the wall and plowed his fingers through his hair. Talk about being an instant husband! Now he was supposed to round up some makeup, and he didn't have a clue as to what he should get. Then he'd have to come up with a nightgown, too.

Dr. Bernie had damn well better be right about not telling that woman the truth.

Marla. He wondered if it was her real name or if he'd heard it entirely wrong. He couldn't go on indefinitely not calling her something. "Honey" seemed a bit too intimate. "Hey, you" or "babe" wouldn't work.

Until he found out otherwise, they were both stuck with Marla.

Meanwhile, his sister would have to help him out. No way was he going to shop for makeup on his own.

"So what's this Marla's coloring like?" Rita asked.

"She's a blond."

"Could you be a bit more specific, little brother? Platinum? Dishwater? What?"

Johnny looked around uncomfortably. After a lot of argument, his sister had agreed to meet him at the local drugstore. Now, standing in the cosmetic aisle, he felt like he'd gotten in way over his head. The array of powders and creams and lipsticks and eye-liners was unending.

"I don't know. Maybe it's a honey-blond with lighter highlights."

"Hmm. Interesting. Definitely interesting." She raised her dark brows suggestively. "What about her complexion?"

Not quite peaches and cream but close. And very smooth. "Fair, I guess."

"Come on, Johnny. You're a cop. You can do better than that."

"All right," he said in disgust, as much at himself as at his sister's innuendos. He knew damn well he'd noticed Marla in more detail than he should, even for a cop. "She's got eyes that hint at being sea-green. Her eyebrows have a slight arch to them and they're a shade darker than the highlights in her hair. Her lips are full but not fat, if you know what I mean." Kiss-able lips, but he didn't want to say that. "And the shape of her face is almost a perfect oval, except where she's got a goose egg on her forehead the size of a baseball. Now what else do you need to know?"

She gave him a curious look. "Tell me again why you're buying this woman, who's a virtual stranger, a whole set of makeup plus nightclothes."

Johnny gritted his teeth. "Because she thinks I'm her husband."

Rita hooted loudly enough that everyone in the store turned around.

"Knock it off, Sis."

"Does Mama know you got married on the sly?"

"I didn't get married. She's lost her memory and thinks—"

"Yeah, right!" She chortled. "Wait till all the girls in town learn somebody snatched you right out from under their noses."

He was going to throttle his sister. Forget he was an officer of the law. Any jury would call it justifiable homicide—particularly a panel of twelve good men.

"Just tell me what kind of makeup she'd want," he said between clenched teeth.

Still strutting and chuckling, Rita picked out a handful of stuff Johnny could barely identify. "A little foundation, an eyebrow pencil, mascara, blush, a couple of shades of lipstick—"

"A couple? Why won't one do?"

"*Pobre* Juan! Poor Johnny. I didn't think you'd be *cheap* with your own wife."

He snatched the makeup from her hands. "I'm gonna get you for this. And don't go telling Mama. She gives me a hard enough time as it is about getting married." And the woman in question this time was already taken. He turned to head for the checkout.

"Wait. You have to get her some cream to take the makeup off at night."

"She can use soap and water like the rest of us," he grumbled.

"Want me to help you pick out a nightgown, too?"

"Forget it. I'll manage that one on my own."

Rita's laughter followed him all the way out of the store. Damn! Sometimes it was hell to have sisters— four of them. But when push came to shove, they were worth more than any amount of money. Not that he was about to admit that to Rita or his other sisters any time soon.

THROUGH THE THROBBING in her head, Marla tried to picture the house where she and Johnny lived. She couldn't.

She couldn't see the outside of the house or any of the rooms. Whenever she tried, she seemed to float into some painful place—high ceilings, exquisite wood floors, expensive appliances in the kitchen. But it hurt too much to be in that place, so her mind bounced her back to the hospital. Stark walls. The smells of floor cleaner and antiseptic. The prodding of nurses taking her temperature and pricking her finger.

The only place where she felt anchored was in Johnny's dark eyes.

Stupidly, she'd had to ask his—her—last name. *Fuentes.* Mr. and Mrs. Johnny Fuentes. It had a nice ring to it.

In her mind, she penned her signature. She liked the way it looked. *Marla Fuentes.* An *F* could be a lovely, dramatic letter—big and bold like the man.

She should have known he'd played football. Though not terribly tall, his shoulders were broad, his arms strong, his hips lean. And his hands were gentle, his fingers blunt with close-clipped nails. She remembered that.

And of all the things she'd forgotten or couldn't imagine, she could almost feel Johnny's hands caressing her intimately. Despite her advanced pregnancy, she longed for the touch of his loving hands on her—everywhere. Probably a case of raging hormones, she decided with a painful chuckle that pulled hard on her bruised ribs.

Why hadn't he kissed her this morning? That question had troubled her all day. Perhaps she'd simply looked too awful. From the glance she'd had of herself in the mirror, she could understand that. But she still wished he had.

He had a nice mouth, with that crooked smile and straight white teeth. A very kissable man.

She shifted in the bed, then moaned as her head pounded and her ribs rebelled once again. If only she could remember where they lived and how they'd met...

JOHNNY FELT LIKE he was smuggling contraband into the hospital in the big Kmart sack he was carrying. He tried to duck past the admissions clerk in the lobby, but she spotted him and waved. He waved back with the bouquet of gladiolus, snapdragons and daisies in his hand.

Shoot, Marla didn't have anybody else to bring her flowers. No woman ought to be stuck in a hospital without something to brighten up her room.

He rapped his knuckles on her open door before stepping inside. The smile she gave him would have brought a weaker man to his knees.

"You brought flowers." She had a lilt to her voice that was pure, unadulterated joy.

"I figured you deserved them after what you've been through."

She lifted her arms for them. "Glads are one of my favorites. But you knew that, didn't you?"

"Yeah, I guess." She looked so pleased he didn't want to tell her they were about the only thing Kmart had. He put the bag on the bed beside her. "Here's the other stuff you wanted. I'll go see if the nurses have a vase or something."

She grasped his arm. "At least let me give you a thank-you kiss before you go running off."

His spine stiffened. "A kiss?" That was more than he'd bargained for.

"Silly. Bend down here."

He wasn't going to panic. He'd kissed plenty of women. But he didn't normally go around kissing married women. Particularly one who thought she was married to *him.*

Her lips were as soft as he'd expected. And warm. Dangerously feminine. Their shape seemed to fit his without any apparent effort, as though they had kissed like this a thousand times before. He wanted to take the kiss deeper, linger a while, taste her more fully. An unnerving spark kindled low in his gut. He wanted this woman. Married or not. Pregnant with another man's child, wearing his diamond ring. It didn't matter.

But it damn well should.

With a force of will, he broke the kiss and cleared his throat. "Marla, I'm going to get a vase now."

Her eyes big and wide and very green, she nodded.

That she'd been affected by the kiss, too, was obvious. That shouldn't be, Johnny thought wildly. She should have known he wasn't her husband, sensed it in a thousand different ways that had nothing to do with amnesia. He knew he could take the biggest whack on the head possible and he'd still remember the feel of Marla's lips on his.

Which was a damn crazy thing to think as he whirled and marched out the door.

Marla exhaled the breath that had lodged in her lungs. The kiss had been almost chaste, yet heat had rocketed through her. And sweet wanting. Then Johnny had raced from the room as though her touch frightened him.

For her, though she diligently searched the dark memory banks of her mind, that had been the first kiss she could recall. She'd wanted to savor it, to make it last.

Obviously, Johnny remembered a good many other kisses and probably not all of them hers.

She twisted the ring on her finger, an exquisite, extravagant diamond set in platinum. Hadn't they been happy together? Was that the problem? Was that why he'd been surprised by her request for a kiss? She felt so close to him—so safe—and he'd been so kind to her, how could they be having marital problems?

She vowed to make amends if she'd been the one to create stress in their marriage. Setting aside any past difficulties meant they could go forward without carrying along any excess baggage. It would be like starting over again.

She smiled at the thought, deciding she liked the idea of courting Johnny Fuentes. And of him courting her.

Opening the sack he'd brought her, she was surprised by the contents—a new nightgown and unopened makeup. She looked up when he returned to the room.

"You didn't have to buy me everything new. Whatever I had at home would've been fine."

Moving the dinner tray out of the way, Johnny placed the vase of flowers on the bed table. "I thought you'd like something fresh."

"That was very sweet of you. And the flowers are lovely. You're too good to me, Johnny."

"Don't be too sure until you check that I got all the stuff you wanted." Self-consciously, he fussed with the blooms, rearranging them. This being a stand-in husband was damn hard work, particularly when he didn't want to take advantage of the situation. "Looks like you didn't eat much dinner. You want me to get you something else? A hamburger, maybe?"

"I don't have much of an appetite. It's the headache, I think."

Turning back to her, he winced at the remnants of her shiner. "Still in a lot of pain?"

She nodded. "The doctor says that will last a while."

"You have to keep up your energy, though. For the baby's sake."

"I know." Sitting up, she swung her legs over the side of the bed. "Could you close the door? I want to change out of this awful hospital gown and put the new one on."

His eyes widened. Good God! She was going to change clothes right in front of him. And he didn't dare look. As he pushed the door shut, he swallowed hard. "Do you need some help?"

"No, I think I can manage."

He stared at the closed door, reading the notice pasted there about escape routes in case of a fire. Behind him, the plastic bag rattled. In spite of his best efforts to block his thoughts, he pictured her naked. Her breasts would be full in anticipation of nursing her baby, delicate blue veins etching her pale skin. Her belly would be swollen and smooth. At the apex of her thighs—

She groaned. "Oh, my..."

Forgetting modesty, he turned and hurried to her, counting his blessings that she was fully covered by the new nightgown. The brushed cotton wasn't even see-through, though it conformed to her distinctively pregnant figure. She was standing beside the bed, her hand on the side rail.

"What's wrong?" he asked, taking her arm to steady her. "You dizzy?"

"No, the baby just let me have it again. Now I think she's practicing to kick field goals. Maybe we shouldn't have mentioned you played football." She smiled at him and took his hand, placing it on her belly. "Here. Feel."

The sense of intimacy was extraordinary. Johnny had observed his sisters during their pregnancies, but he'd never actually felt a baby move inside its mother before. A foot or a tiny little fist pressed against his palm, almost like it was saying hello.

"Can you feel her?" Marla asked.

"Yeah." A lump formed in Johnny's throat. The little kid in there needed a daddy and it was his job to find that man, reunite him with his wife and child. But he was as envious as hell that some other man had the right to hold this woman in his arms and cradle her baby.

Lifting his head, he met Marla's gaze. As he'd hoped, the light green nightgown he'd bought matched her eyes and it was like looking out at the ocean on a day when the sun caught the waves. This woman needed a man to protect her, to care for her, and so did her baby. Because he'd been the one to find her on the beach, she'd become his responsibility. In some ways, that was scarier than his stint with the Los Angeles Police Department, where he'd been expected to face down a gang of punk kids armed to the teeth. But he couldn't turn his back on her any more than he'd been able to run from the danger of a gang rumble.

His connection to Marla and her baby was becoming so strong, he wasn't sure he'd ever be able to sever it even after she recognized their make-believe marriage was a charade.

The baby moved again, nestling her tiny fist in his palm. Johnny's throat constricted. He understood why his mother was so eager for him to have a family of his own. It'd be easy to love the baby that was growing in Marla's belly.

"You'll be such a good daddy," she whispered.

"I hope so." She seemed a little unsteady on her feet, so he helped lower her to sit on the edge of the bed. "I don't want you overdoing things, you hear?"

"Not much chance of that," she said wryly. "I'm as weak as a kitten."

"And just as cute."

She wrinkled her nose. "If you don't mind one with a black eye."

"A little makeup and nobody will notice."

Settling back on the bed, she searched through the sack and found the shiny compact he'd purchased. As she fussed with her makeup, Johnny busied himself checking out the overhead television and the closet for patients' clothing. Only the dress Marla had been wearing on the beach and her shoes were there, plus the limp polka-dot scarf that had been knotted around her neck.

Marla brushed a little color on her cheeks, staring critically at the stranger she saw in the mirror. Her eyes were a little too bright, her complexion pale except for the purpling bruise around her left eye.

Marla. She tested the name again, struggling to make a connection between the woman she saw in the mirror and some small bit of her past. *Who* are *you, Marla Fuentes?* she asked the image.

Whoever she was, she wanted to look as good as possible for Johnny. He was her blue knight, the one who'd rescued her, who knew her best. He'd help her through this ordeal. She simply had to keep faith in him. Her husband.

A wave of dizziness washed over her and her hand trembled. All she had to do was believe in Johnny. He'd make sure everything would be all right. Thank goodness she'd remembered his face. That positive thought seemed to lessen the apprehension that had been pressing at the back of her skull for hours. Or had it been days?

Finally, she announced, "I'm afraid that's the best repair job I can do."

Johnny turned toward her, smiled and said, "Beautiful." He meant it. Rita had done a good job of selecting the right colors for Marla, sight unseen. Her cheeks had taken on a healthy glow and her eyes looked wider, her lashes longer. "You'll be a regular Sleeping Beauty tonight."

"Thank you. For everything. I feel almost human again."

She looked it, too. Temptingly so. "Look, I've gotta go. I, uh, haven't had dinner yet and—"

"Oh, Johnny, I'm sorry. I wasn't even thinking."

"You let me do the thinking for now. Your job is to rest and get well as fast as you can." As naturally as he could, he bent to place a quick kiss on her lips. While he was at it, he gingerly picked up the compact and slipped it into his pocket, replacing it with a second identical one.

His job was to discover who this woman was, not to get involved with her. Tracing her fingerprints was his best chance to discover her real identity.

Somehow the prospect of handing her over to her husband held less appeal than it should.

Federal Building, San Francisco

"WHAT DO YOU MEAN, she's gone?" The assistant U.S. attorney glared at the two postal inspectors, her narrow face and hooked nose reminding Tommy Tompkins of the Wicked Witch of the West in Oz.

Tommy shoved his hands into his trouser pockets, making his jacket bunch up over his wrists. "She sold the house and moved out. The place is empty."

"Haven't you been keeping an eye on her?"

"We were busy collecting evidence, in case you've forgotten," his partner, Hal Donovan, said.

"I'm going to the grand jury tomorrow morning to ask for an indictment. Grand theft mail fraud. I want that woman found."

Tommy shrugged. "We're checking with the airlines."

Her eyes narrowed. The toughest prosecutor on the West Coast, she had a conviction rate high enough to make the Mafia flinch. A crook working alone didn't stand a prayer of getting off the hook.

"You think she's fled the country?" the prosecutor asked.

"She's got a passport. We figure she has money stashed somewhere out of our reach."

"How about a forwarding address? You gentlemen do work for the postal system. Did you check?" Her tone was condescending, her features pinched.

"She didn't file one," Hal said, ignoring the gibe. "Sometimes people don't do that right away."

The prosecutor picked up the reading glasses from her desk and placed them securely on her nose. "Find her. She's got a lot of victims out there and they're beginning to scream bloody murder about getting their money back." Effectively ending the conversation, she dragged a thick file from the stack on her desk and began to read the contents.

Tommy met Hal's gaze, and they both shook their heads. It was easy enough for the prosecutor to order them to find a suspect. Doing it when the woman had evidently gone into hiding or fled the country was a whole different matter.

But if and when they caught the suspect, the prosecutor was going to nail the woman but good. The case was rock solid. At a minimum, she was going to spend the next twenty-five years in a federal penitentiary.

If it had been Tommy, he would have run, too.

Chapter Three

"Lynel, have you gotten a report back on those fingerprints I wanted you to trace?"

It had been two days since Johnny had handed over the compact to the department's fingerprint technician. Meanwhile, he'd locked up a teenager who'd been mugging tourists, testified in another case at the court in San Luis Obispo and visited Marla. That part of his job had been the hardest.

She'd been asking when she could come home. So far, both he and Dr. Bernie had put her off. As her strength returned, postponing her release from the hospital would become increasingly difficult to explain. Lying didn't come easily to Johnny.

The technician shoved himself back from his computer. As usual, every level space in his office was filled with books, papers and assorted police paraphernalia. A pair of tennis shoes—once thought to be evidence from an old crime scene—was sitting on top of the computer.

"Word came back this morning from the FBI. No record they can find. DMV is still working on it, but the thumbprint isn't very clear, too cut up. I'm not optimistic we'll get a match.''

At least they could be pretty sure she wasn't a fleeing felon with a convenient memory lapse, he thought with relief. ''How 'bout missing person reports? Anything?''

''The only thing new is a couple of missing teens. Probably runaways.''

Marla didn't meet that description. ''Okay. Keep an eye out for me and let me know if you hear anything at all.''

''Will do, Chief.''

Struggling to figure out what to do next, Johnny headed for his office. Patty was on days this week at the dispatcher's desk.

''How's your *wife* getting along?'' she asked, grinning.

''My bachelor days aren't over yet, Grandma.'' He purposefully eyed the row of family pictures lining a nearby shelf, each one featuring a different grandchild. You'd never know by looking at Patty that she'd been eligible for retirement six years ago but had refused to give up her job. She knew so much about the town and everyone who lived in it, he'd hate to lose her.

She snorted at him. ''Will be soon enough, I'd guess, the way you're spending so much time at the hospital.''

''She's all alone, Patty. What am I supposed to do? Leave her feeling abandoned?''

"Some men would, Johnny. But not you. That's why everybody loves you so much."

"Yeah, right. And here I thought they loved me 'cause they don't want me to give them speeding tickets." He laughed and went into his office.

Right on top of his desk was a message from Dr. Bernie. He wanted to see Johnny ASAP. Nothing on the pink slip of paper said why.

Johnny's gut clenched. Maybe Marla's memory had returned on its own. The doctor had said that could happen at any time.

Drawing a deep breath, he said, "So be it." At least the mystery would be solved.

He made a couple of quick calls to confirm a meeting with the local disaster preparedness group and scheduled one of his new officers into a training class in Sacramento. In thirty minutes, he was in Dr. Bernie's office at the hospital.

"I'm going to have to discharge Marla," he said.

"Has she regained her memory?"

"No."

"Then how can you discharge her? Where would she go? She's not strong enough to be on her own yet." In addition to not having any money or credit or any possibility of getting a job in her condition.

"Social services is working on that problem. But administration says she has to go. Frankly, there's no medical reason for her to stay. Periodic follow-ups with a neurologist and regular visits to her OB/GYN should be enough. And without insurance—"

"The bean counters are throwing her out."

"It's a reasonable decision to make." The doctor came around to the front of his desk and leaned back against it, crossing his ankles and arms. His stethoscope was hooked around his neck. "There's a battered-women's facility in town that may be able to take her, but the director is dragging her feet because Marla isn't actually a victim of domestic violence—so far as we know. The other choice is a homeless shelter in San Luis Obispo."

"Terrific. And then what is she going to do? Have her baby on some cot with a bunch of drunks and down-on-their-luck vagrants playing midwife."

"I think we ought to consider another option."

"I'm all for that. What?"

"You taking her home with you."

Johnny felt that same sinking sensation he'd had when the doctor had announced Marla thought he was her husband. Only now it was far worse. He knew her. He cared about her. And was absolutely certain he'd never be able to carry off the charade of being her husband without getting himself *and* her into very deep trouble.

"I can't do it."

"I understand, but I had hoped—"

"Dammit, Doc, I can't get involved with every stray woman that shows up in town. I have a life of my own to lead."

"Absolutely."

"She'd never buy it anyway. Once I got her home, she'd know she'd never lived there. Hell, my house isn't much more than a beach cottage. From the way she acts and that monster ring on her finger, I'd bet dollars to doughnuts she's never lived in a place that small in her life unless it was on vacation."

"That may well be true."

"And how would I explain there's none of her stuff there? Tell me that, huh?"

"Based on her MRI and the other tests we've given her, I suspect her amnesia is only partially related to her physical trauma."

"You mean she's faking it?"

"No, not at all. Her memory loss is quite real and, I'm sure, very disturbing as well as somewhat selective at times. Her condition means she will be more accepting of inconsistencies than others would be under similar circumstances."

"You mean if I took her home, she'd *believe* that she and I are actually married and we'd always lived there?"

"She appears to be quite attached to you."

Johnny was attached to her, too, but that wasn't the point. "And just what am I supposed to do if she expects us to..." Heat stole up his neck. "Dammit, Doc, I'm not a saint. And I'm not her husband, either."

The hint of a smile curled Dr. Bernie's lips. "I think we can avoid that problem by making it clear, given her accident and her advanced pregnancy, sexual activity would be dangerous for both her and the baby. Not that a husband and wife can't enjoy each other right up to the eleventh hour if they're careful. But under the circumstances..." He shrugged. "I think it's safe to say I can, in good conscience, discourage that kind of activity.''

Johnny wasn't sure if he felt relief or disappointment and tried not to think about what that meant. Except that he was seriously contemplating doing what the doctor suggested—taking Marla home with him. And he was a fool to even be considering the idea.

"Look, assuming I agree to do this, she's still bound to ask questions about our past. Lots of them. How the hell am I supposed to respond?''

"Be vague, if you can. You could even tell her it's better if her memories return on their own without your prodding. In fact, it wouldn't be wise to implant incorrect memories at this stage. Her confusion might deepen. We wouldn't want that.''

"No, we wouldn't,'' Johnny grumbled. Be vague? Hell, his mother had always told him when he lied it showed up like neon on his face.

He paced across the room and stared out the window at the parking lot. It was a typical summer day, blue sky, a breeze blowing and the temperature around seventy degrees. He wondered why anyone would want to live anywhere but here.

"My mother's a pretty terrific lady,'' he said thoughtfully. "She's always got room for one more at her house. Maybe she could—''

"In my discussions with social services we considered finding a local family for her to stay with, at least until the baby arrives. I'm reluctant, however.''

"Why?'' He turned back to the doctor.

"I still believe the wisest course for my patient is the return of her memory in its own good time, without being forced in any way. For her health and that of the baby's, the best option is for you to continue to assume the role of her husband. If we place her in any other environment, the shock might set her recovery back by months."

"You sure know how to lay on the guilt, Doc."

"I was raised by a good Catholic mother. Weren't you?"

"Yeah, tell me about it." Did he have a choice? Not really, not if he was going to be able to look himself in the mirror tomorrow morning, knowing he'd sent Marla off to some homeless shelter where she didn't know a soul and would be scared to death. But if he was going to make this work, he needed some time to get organized. "Give me a couple of hours, Doc. Till this afternoon, so I can get things ready for her."

Dr. Bernie nodded as though he'd known all along that Johnny would agree to the arrangement. And he probably had. In spite of being a cop and the chief of police, Johnny Fuentes had always had "good guy" written all over his face. Damned if he could change his stripes now.

But being a good guy meant he couldn't mess with another man's wife.

BORED WITH WATCHING talk shows and not interested in the soaps, Marla switched off the TV and struggled to sit up. If she didn't get out of this hospital pretty soon, she'd lose more than her memory. Her sanity would go, too.

She sighed and tried to keep the panic at bay. Whenever she thought of the past, all she found was a black empty hole as if she'd only existed somewhere in outer space until her accident. No images of friends or family came to her. No sense of where she'd been raised or gone to school. There was simply nothing for her to cling to.

She didn't even know what kind of person she'd been. What if she'd been a terrible woman and that's why no one except Johnny had visited her?

Dr. Bernie had told her to be patient. That was easier said than done. Particularly when twice she'd had dreams so filled with grief and heartbreak that she'd awakened crying.

But she didn't know why.

Awkwardly levering herself up, she walked to the window and automatically searched the parking lot for Johnny's car. The doctor had said he'd be discharging her this afternoon. Perhaps when she got home, the familiarity of her own things around her would trigger memories. She certainly hoped so.

Someone knocked on the door.

"Hi. Marla?"

The woman was about Marla's age and was carrying some clothes on hangers and a small paper bag. She had long, dark hair, friendly brown eyes and a smile that was vaguely familiar.

"I'm sorry. Do I know you?" Marla asked.

"I'm Johnny's sister, Rita Diaz."

"Oh." Now that she'd said that, Marla immediately saw the family resemblance. "This is so embarrassing. I know I should have recognized—"

"Don't worry about it. Johnny explained what happened. He's just happy you and the baby are going to be okay." She glanced at Marla's protruding belly and smiled again. "Looks like you're about ready to pop. The last month of my pregnancies, I've always felt like a beached whale."

"You have children?"

"Three little darlings and every one of them more trouble than the next."

"I wish I could remember them."

"Trust me on this, honey." Rita's happy laughter rippled around the room, inviting anyone within hearing distance to join in the fun. "Some things are better forgotten."

In spite of her lack of memory, Marla felt an instant affinity for her sister-in-law. More than anything, she wanted them to be friends.

"Here." Rita handed her the clothes. "Johnny asked me to bring these by so you could change before your grand escape from this joint. He said the dress you were wearing when you had the accident is a mess."

"And stiff as a board. It looks like I went swimming in the ocean with it."

"That's what he thinks happened all right."

Marla, clothes in hand, stepped into the small bathroom to change. Like everything else in her severely limited world, the maternity blouse and slacks didn't

look the least bit familiar, and the bright colors didn't
seem like those she might normally select. But the
bra fit her full breasts and the stretchy undies were
certainly the right size...for a whale. Idly, she wondered what her figure had been like eight months
ago...and if she'd ever see herself that way again.

She pressed her hand to her belly and her chin
trembled. "You've got cousins, babykins. Won't that
be fun?" She wondered where her cousins were, or
if she'd ever had any.

A new wave of despair washed over her. Then she
remembered she'd soon be going home with Johnny,
her husband. And she had a terrific sister-in-law who
seemed willing to be her friend.

Lots of people in this world had less than that, she
assured herself.

"I CAN'T TELL YOU how good it is to be out of that
hospital. I can even smell the ocean," Marla said as
Johnny helped her out of the wheelchair and into his
waiting car, the high seat of the four-wheel-drive vehicle giving her trouble because of her girth. She
grunted.

"You okay?" Johnny asked.

"Fine, for a beached whale."

Rita laughed and handed Marla the sack they'd
stuffed with her nightgown and dirty clothes. The
wilting bouquet of flowers had already been placed in
the back seat.

"You take care, you hear?" Rita urged.

"I will. Come see me?" Marla tried to keep the

pleading note from her voice. She so much needed a friend.

Rita flashed a look at Johnny. "Sure. I'll drop by soon."

"And bring the children."

"That wife of yours is a glutton for punishment, Johnny. You'd better take good care of her."

"I'll do my best." He shut the passenger door, told his sister goodbye and went around to the driver's side. "Buckle up," he said as he got in.

"Absolutely. The doctor told me that's what saved my life in the accident." She extended the belt and snapped it in place. "By the way, what happened to my car?"

"We haven't found it yet."

"That's odd." She closed her eyes, trying to picture the car she'd been driving...and where she'd been. All she saw was a confusion of images—mangled cars, long limousines and a motorcycle officer. She swallowed the fear that rose in her throat. Her head began to throb and she shoved the image aside. "How far away do we live?"

He turned left out of the parking lot and headed down the hill. "A couple of miles. We have to drive through town."

That was good. Maybe she'd see something she recognized—a store where she'd shopped, familiar faces on the street. Her fingers tightened around the door handle. Her memory *had* to come back soon. Except for Johnny, she felt so lost and alone.

It was his image that gave her comfort when panic

threatened. He was such a solid man. Perhaps it was his square jaw or the slight bend of his nose—as if it had once been broken—that made Marla confident Johnny could protect her from any danger.

But it was his crooked smile and his dark, caring eyes that made her heart stumble whenever she saw him.

Sighing, she glanced out of the car windows.

What appeared to be the main street of town had angle parking and shops that appealed to the tourists strolling along the sidewalks. Art galleries sat side by side with T-shirt stores, craft shops, lunch delis and real estate offices. A store featuring miniature lead figures had an intriguing sign reading Dream Man Collection pasted across the front window. She smiled, thinking Johnny certainly qualified as her personal dream man, her blue knight. He wouldn't betray her.

But nothing along the street looked familiar. Not the stores and certainly not any of the people Marla saw. She began to tremble and clasped her hands tightly together. Dear God, why couldn't she remember *anything?*

Reaching across the front seat, Johnny covered her clenched hands with his. "Easy, kitten. You're going to squeeze the life out of the baby."

Kitten? Had he always called her that? It sounded so loving, so affectionate, she wanted that to be true. And it made her want to curl up in Johnny's arms and purr. But for the life of her, she couldn't remember ever having a nickname before.

The road dipped beneath Highway 1 and came out in an older residential neighborhood with tiny houses set on narrow lots, many of them with ocean views. Johnny pulled into the driveway of one of those whose back faced the ocean. Marla willed her damaged memory to work, to recognize the white clapboard house with its slightly peeling paint and small redwood porch.

Nothing. Absolutely nothing came to her.

"We, uh, only moved in recently," Johnny said. "I'm still trying to get the place fixed up. But the view is terrific."

"It's fine." It seemed so small, not like... The image of a Tudor-style house with a rolling front lawn popped into her mind. The pain that came with it, sharp and cutting, shattered the picture, nearly taking her breath away. She couldn't think about that place, didn't want to. The agony was too great to face. Stubbornly, she squelched the panic that rose in her throat.

"The house will probably seem strange to you at first. That's what the doc said. Try not to let that bother you."

"I won't." She'd far rather be here with Johnny than in that other place.... She tried for a smile. "I'm just glad to be home."

"Yeah." He got out and helped her down.

The sea breeze caught her hair and teased it across her face. Inhaling deeply of the tangy salt air and feeling the warm sun on her cheeks, she laughed. "This is heavenly. I can't imagine living anywhere else."

He gave her an odd look as he placed his palm at the small of her back and escorted her inside. The heat of his hand felt warm. Protective. She cherished the unaccustomed feeling of security.

What she found inside the house was no more familiar to her than the exterior had been. A small living room, sparsely furnished, and a kitchen that looked out over the ocean. Only the view from the windows at the back of the house calmed her. Watching the steady roll of the waves toward the beach comforted her, as did the subdued grays and blues and greens of the sky and ocean. Here she could be happy. And secure.

"If you're up to it later, we can take a walk along the beach."

"Yes, the doctor said I should walk every day if I'm able."

"Great."

She spied the white brick fireplace, the narrow mantel lined with trophies. "What's all this?" she asked, crossing the room to examine them.

"Nothing, really. I enter a couple of local triathlons every year."

"Looks like you've been pretty successful." She noted two firsts and a second-place finish. More than successful, she'd say, and understood now why Johnny appeared to be in such superb condition.

As though he were embarrassed by his athletic prowess, he said, "Come take a look at the bedroom. Then maybe you ought to rest a while."

She'd been resting for longer than she liked. The

inactivity, like her loss of memory, grated on Marla. Her fingers itched to get busy decorating the house, finding just the right paintings for the bare walls, adding a flounce over the picture window.

She mentally paused. Why hadn't she already gotten to work on such an exciting task as decorating her own home? Had her pregnancy slowed her down that much? Or was she just plain lazy?

Lord help her, she was afraid to ask, instinctively knowing there were some answers she did not want to hear.

Before Johnny left her alone in the bedroom to rest, she took his hand. "Thank you," she said.

"For what?"

"For bringing me home."

His deep brown eyes caressed her face and he brought one finger to her lips as if to quiet her. "You're welcome, kitten. You have a good nap, okay?"

His touch was like a kiss but all too brief. A swift longing for more arrowed through her, centering low in her body. Her heart lurched as disappointment battled with desire. Home or not, the doctor had said making love was off-limits. Her raging hormones would simply have to calm down or at least she couldn't act on her wishes. That wouldn't be fair to Johnny—to encourage more than she could deliver.

The door closed behind him as he left.

Restless, she wandered around the room, running her fingers over the top of the oak chest of drawers, feeling the texture of the bright quilt on the double bed, hoping that the tactile experience of being home would somehow jar her memory back.

She opened the closet door and examined the clothes hanging there next to Johnny's uniforms and casual slacks and shirts. What few things she had were all maternity clothes, colorful outfits that made her smile. She must have been truly proud of being pregnant when she bought those. No question, the whole world would notice her condition when she wore them.

But where were her other clothes?

Confusion rose in her like the tide and nibbled away at her unsteady hold on reality. Why couldn't she recall the answer to such an ordinary question? She hadn't been pregnant all her life. What had she worn before?

And why did she have the troubling feeling that life had begun the day Johnny rescued her?

JOHNNY COULDN'T concentrate on the work he'd brought home from the office. He'd spread the papers out on the kitchen table and booted up his laptop computer, but he kept glancing at the bouquet of flowers he'd brought home from the hospital and stuck in an empty milk carton. After three days, they looked a lot worse for wear. He would have left them at the hospital, but Marla had insisted he bring them along.

He was all she had.

He wondered what it must be like to wake up one morning and not know another single soul in the world. Just the thought scared him. A woman as soft and vulnerable as Marla must have been terrified.

But she hadn't panicked. That had cost her plenty. He'd seen the tears threaten as she struggled with her confusion. She hadn't given in. At least not in front of him. Being strong like that took a helluva lot of courage.

He plugged away at the reports for an hour, then gave up the effort. He stretched, then stood and decided to start dinner. There was some ground meat and wilted lettuce in the refrigerator. He'd try for tacos.

With the meat sizzling in the frying pan, he didn't hear her come up behind him. The first thing he knew, her arms were wrapped around his middle and her cheek was resting on his back. Her light feminine scent surrounded him.

"Handsome, and he cooks, too," she teased. "How did I get lucky enough to marry you?"

He stiffened, trying to halt the sensual heat that thrummed through his body. This was another man's wife. But he could feel the press of her breasts below his shoulder blades, the swell of her pregnancy against his butt and the loving sensation of her arms around him.

He turned, intending to ease her away from him. But when he saw the plea in her eyes, the need in their depths, he couldn't do that. So he gave her a quick, reassuring hug in return. Or that's what he'd meant to do. Instead, he found himself kissing her, tasting her full lips. She welcomed him with a sigh, opening to him without any encouragement. Her tongue lightly brushed against his, sending a jolt of unadulterated lust through him.

Dammit! He couldn't do this.

"Marla..." His voice was thick. "We can't do this."

"I know. I just needed to..." Her words trailed off and she looked away. "I'm sure I'll feel good enough tomorrow to handle the cooking. You work all day. You shouldn't have to cook, too."

"Don't worry about it, kitten." He smoothed the back of his hand along her cheek. So sleek, so soft. "You don't have to do anything you don't feel up to. We can always order Chinese."

"Of course." Marla frowned, the stitches pulling tight on her forehead. She didn't really like Chinese. Oh, fried rice and sweet and sour were fine, but usually the chow mein was too salty. How did she know one of her least favorite foods, she wondered, and Johnny didn't? Hadn't she told him?

He served up dinner and they ate at the kitchen table in front of the big picture window. Marla noticed the surf rolling in and a bank of clouds edging closer to the beach. Thinking about the approaching fog, she shivered and quickly tried to find a new topic of conversation.

"Johnny, where are my clothes? The ones I wore before I turned into an oversize mammal?"

He coughed, choking on his third taco.

"Are you all right?"

"Fine." He coughed again and cleared his throat.

His eyes teared. "I guess you figured you wouldn't be needing them for a while."

"They're in storage?"

"Right." He took a big gulp of milk. "In storage."

That seemed logical. But she tried to picture boxing up all her clothes and simply couldn't. There'd been plenty of room in the closet for them. Her mind seemed as dense as the approaching fog bank. And whenever she penetrated the gray mist, her head began to pound as if a chorus of bass drummers had taken up residence.

She was better off not thinking about the past. The present—her husband and her unborn child—was all that mattered.

She held that thought as she and Johnny walked together along the beach after dinner and as she got ready for bed. Then she discovered he was planning to sleep in the guest bedroom across the hall.

That revelation hurt. Granted, she understood they couldn't have sex. The doctor had made it clear that wasn't a good idea. But she desperately wanted to be near him. He was her touchstone, her anchor.

As she lay in the double bed alone, thinking about the single bed Johnny slept in and the empty bedroom she'd discovered down the hall, the dark seemed to press in on her. The silence. Fears bubbled and frothed like waves battering the beach, stealing her underpinnings of sanity. Images flitted through her head in disconnected bits and pieces. Memories or imagination, she couldn't tell which.

The fear of being alone, of never being held again

by someone she loved, rose in her with such force, she leaped out of bed. Her legs were shaking, her heart thundering in her chest.

She couldn't be alone. Not tonight. Not in her own home where everything, even the creak of wood and the hum of the sea, felt so unfamiliar.

Something was definitely wrong, *terribly* wrong with the way she felt. With her fears. With the memories she'd lost.

Cradling her belly, she staggered toward the bedroom door and made her way blindly to the room opposite hers. The door was opened a crack.

"Johnny!"

She heard him shift on the bed. "Huh?" he asked groggily.

"I know we can't..." She gulped down a sob. "Please, I don't want to be alone. Sleep with me, Johnny. Just hold me." *So I don't have to face the past alone.*

Chapter Four

Johnny squeezed his eyes shut.

He didn't need this. Temptation wasn't something he handled well. Marla was all the things he wanted and hadn't yet found—a beautiful woman, soft and vulnerable with an inner strength. A woman with an instinctive capacity for love. A woman who'd be a good mother to his children.

But she wore another man's ring and was pregnant with that man's child.

"Please..." She whispered her plea more softly this time, with an even greater depth of feeling. Of need.

He couldn't refuse her. She thought he was her husband. "I'm coming." He rolled out of bed, grateful he'd had enough foresight to wear pajama bottoms tonight instead of sleeping buck naked as he usually did.

"I'm sorry."

"Shh. It's all right. You need your sleep."

Resting his hand on the back of her neck beneath the soft fall of her silky hair, he gently urged her toward the master bedroom. She got into bed and he climbed in from the opposite side. He nearly groaned aloud as she turned her back, spooning her hips against his groin. Automatically, he looped his arm across her midsection, feeling the swell of her belly.

"After the baby comes," she whispered, "I'll make it up to you that we couldn't…"

"After the baby," he murmured, echoing her words. In spite of himself, he rubbed his cheek against her sweet-smelling hair, the scent herbal and feminine. By the time the baby arrived, Marla would be back in the arms of her husband. He'd be the one to pleasure her body and receive pleasure in return. And Johnny would be sleeping alone again.

"Johnny, before my accident…were we having problems? I mean marital—"

"No problems, kitten." Keep his answers vague, the doctor had told him. Let Marla discover the past for herself. "Just go to sleep."

She nestled more tightly against him and rested her hand on his, toying with his fingers. "You make me feel so safe."

Serve and protect, a police officer's motto. The job had never been more challenging.

"You're safe with me." He gritted his teeth. "I promise."

"I know." A sigh raised her breasts, brushing them again his forearm. "I think I can sleep now. Thank you."

"Great." Johnny didn't think he could say the same for himself. Holding his breath, he tried to ease his hips back from hers. He didn't want her to feel his growing arousal. Their position was too intimate for him not to respond. Predictably, he was responding in spades. He couldn't act on his natural urges. And he didn't want her to feel any guilt because he couldn't—for reasons she didn't know and he couldn't tell her—as per the doctor's orders. Being vague might work for Dr. Bernie, but it sure as hell didn't work for him.

"Hmmm," she said sleepily. "Tomorrow I think we ought to start furnishing the nursery. It won't be long before Caitlin shows up."

Johnny froze. *Caitlin?* Was she talking about the baby? And Marla wanted to furnish the bedroom, the empty one down the hall, in cuddly bears or pink ballerinas? He definitely hadn't counted on that.

Or did she mean she was getting labor pains right now? Damn, he had no idea how to handle that. Well, yeah, he'd had a two-hour class on how to deliver a baby in the back seat of a patrol car. But this would be different. *Very* different. As far as Marla was concerned, he was the kid's father. They hadn't covered that particular complication in the class he'd taken at the LAPD.

He'd managed to drift off to sleep only to be awakened by someone calling his name.

"Juan! Your mama's here, *hijo*. I wanna meet this wife of yours, *sí?*"

He cracked one eye open. Sunlight filtered through the morning overcast outside the bedroom window, casting the ocean view in shades of gray. Groaning, he struggled to sit upright.

Marla's head rested on his chest and their legs were tangled together. She blinked, slowly coming awake, moving her head to the pillow. "What's wrong?"

"My mother's timing, that's what's wrong." First chance, he was going to take the house key away from his mother. Her popping in unexpectedly was not a good thing.

He got to his feet and grabbed a pair of jeans and a shirt from the closet. Hopping from one foot to the other, he tugged on the pants and headed for the front of the house. Having Mama find him in bed with Marla would only confuse the situation.

"There you are, Juan baby." Her arms full of grocery bags, she beamed a smile at him that suffused her wrinkled features with happiness. "So, how come you didn't tell your mama you got yourself a wife, huh?"

"Mama, hush." He hooked his arm through hers and propelled her into the kitchen where Marla wouldn't overhear them. "She's not my wife, Mama. Rita must have told you—"

"*Sí, sí,* I know all about this craziness. But you need a woman and she's gonna have a baby, so it's okay. You'll have a family like—"

"It's another man's baby, Mama. I'm trying to find her husband."

"Bah. She's got no husband or he would have been here by now."

"She's wearing a ring, Mama."

"No matter. Rita says she's a nice lady. You keep her."

Johnny rolled his eyes. Dolores Fuentes had to be the most stubborn, most determined woman in the world when she set her mind on something. He supposed that's how she'd managed to keep her family together after his dad died, but Johnny didn't like it when she focused all her considerable energy on "fixing" his life by matchmaking.

Rita called from the front door, "Give me a hand with this bassinet, Johnny. Mama says we've got to put it—"

"Now wait a minute."

From down the hallway, Marla appeared. She was wearing a bright maternity blouse splashed with red and yellow flowers atop matching red stirrup pants. She'd obviously taken time to run a brush through her hair and dab on a little lipstick.

"Oh, my," she said, spotting the bassinet on the front porch. She fingered the white lace trimming. "It's lovely, Rita. You shouldn't have—"

"Of course we should," Mama said. "All my babies and my grandbabies have slept in that bassinet. My Juan, too. It's—how you say—a family heirloom, *sí?*"

Confusion pulled Marla's brows together, and her gaze flicked from Rita to Johnny's mother.

"This is my mother," Johnny said quickly.

"Here, let me take a look at my daughter-in-law." Dropping the grocery bags filled with baby clothes to the floor, Dolores Fuentes held out her arms to embrace Marla. "Such a pretty girl. You're a lucky boy, Johnny. And she's gonna to be a mama, too."

Without any particular invitation, Dolores hugged Marla, enfolding her in her arms as she did with almost everyone she met. Though an inch or two shorter than Marla, and certainly plumper, his mother showered her make-believe daughter-in-law with the love that came so naturally to her, encompassing the unborn baby in the process. Having successfully raised her own children, Mama longed for endless grandchildren to love.

For a moment, Marla stood rigidly in Dolores's arms, and then she relaxed, succumbing to Dolores like sand in the face of a super high tide. She hugged her back, and Johnny released a tense breath he hadn't realized he'd been holding.

"I'm sorry I can't remember—"

"Pshaw! We'll make new memories. You're one of the family now." She hooked her arm through Marla's. "Rita tells me we're gonna have a little girl."

"Not *we*, Mama. Marla is."

She waved Johnny off as if he were no more than a pesky fly.

"Yes, I thought I'd name her Caitlin," Marla said.

"I always liked Teresa myself. You think about that. Maybe it goes better with Fuentes, *sí?*"

Marla looked a little perplexed.

"Juan, you bring the bassinet. We gotta fix up the nursery for our *bebé.*"

"Mama, we haven't even had our breakfast yet."

"It's in the car. *Huevos rancheros* and *sopaipillas, sí?* Your favorites." She hustled Marla down the hall toward the back bedroom.

His mouth watered. The only thing that made up for his mother's bossiness was her great cooking. With a nod at Rita, he hefted the bassinet and carried it down the hall after his mother. And his *wife*.

MARLA WAS SURE she'd never met a family quite like Johnny's. The three of them all talked at once during breakfast, Mama teasing Johnny about his being such a mischievous child, always getting into trouble and picking on his sisters—one of whom was still in college, Marla gathered, while the other two had moved away with their husbands and children. Johnny defended himself good-naturedly, insisting he'd been the victim of the all-female household.

No wonder Johnny was so comfortable with her, and probably around all women. A man who grew up with four sisters must certainly have learned early how to deal with the opposite sex. And his mother and sister seemed to dote on him. Apparently, from a young age, he'd been the only man in the family.

Mostly, Marla simply listened to the conversation flowing around her and wondered how she could possibly have forgotten this incredible feeling of family. The warmth was like the sun breaking through the morning clouds, welcoming her.

She smiled at Johnny across the table. *Her husband.* Gratitude welled up in her. Surely she must be the luckiest woman in the world.

After they'd all left—including Johnny, who'd gone for a Saturday morning run—Marla sat Buddha-style on the floor of the nursery sorting through the hand-me-down infant clothes Rita had brought. She lifted a tiny cotton undershirt to her cheek, feeling its soft caress, and stroked a fluffy lamb's tail on a terry-cloth sleeper. She wanted so much to give her baby everything she could possibly need.

But most of all, she wanted to give her baby all the love a child could ever absorb.

A feeling of emptiness stole over her. Had she been loved as a child with the fierce protectiveness Dolores Fuentes displayed for her children? Marla didn't think so. If she had been, no amount of damage to her skull would have made her forget the feeling.

Where were her parents? she wondered. And why couldn't she find even a trace of their memory in her mind?

When she'd finished looking at the baby clothes, she showered, gingerly washing her hair, and was dressed again by the time Johnny returned.

"How'd it go?" she asked.

"Had a good run this morning." Giving her one of his patented smiles, he plowed his fingers through his sweat-dampened hair, shifting the dark strands back from his broad forehead. The gray LAPD T-shirt he wore was sleeveless and ripped off at the midriff; his nylon running shorts revealed muscular legs. Overall, the picture of Johnny standing in his living room was a very appealing one of an athlete in his prime.

Marla warmed at the thought of being his wife.

"I was thinking about walking into town," she said. "For my dose of exercise."

"Great. I'll go with you."

"You don't have to. It isn't far, is it?"

He cocked his head, studying her. "You're just out of the hospital. Let's say I'd feel better if I went along with you."

Marla could hardly argue with his reasoning, but she hated to be a burden. "If you're sure."

"Give me a chance to shower and I'll be ready to go."

THE SKIES HAD CLEARED and a gentle breeze blew in from the ocean. Though a headache still niggled at the back of Marla's head, it felt good to be out and moving, even if a little awkwardly with her oversize tummy leading the way. Smiling, she slipped her hand into Johnny's. She felt him flinch in surprise before taking hold.

"This is such a pretty area," she said, puzzled why he'd reacted that way. She felt such enormous pride walking beside him and couldn't resist a casual touch.

"The houses are pretty small."

The image of a much larger house came to her, a virtual mansion, and she shivered at the wave of loneliness that swept over her. "Most families don't need more than this." Not if they shared the kind of love the Fuentes family did.

"A lot of women couldn't be happy here," Johnny commented.

"Fortunately, I'm not one of them."

He gave her a curious look as they stepped off a curb to cross the street. Dressed casually, he was wearing hip-hugging jeans and a pale blue T-shirt stenciled BAKER TO VEGAS RUN, 1995, LAPD, no doubt a souvenir from one of his athletic endeavors.

There weren't many twists and turns on the way to town. Mar del Oro wasn't all that big a place. She'd be able to come again on her own without getting lost, she was sure.

Once they reached the business section, they strolled along, enjoying the displays in the windows and doing a little people-watching. From time to time, she caught a glimpse of someone she thought she recognized only to realize when they got closer that they were strangers. And no one in town acknowledged her. It was as though she'd only recently arrived from outer space. She wondered how that could possibly be. Hadn't she made a single friend in town?

In contrast, Johnny knew almost everyone who wasn't a tourist. They smiled and waved, glancing at Marla with open curiosity. A prickle of unease teased along her spine. She was the one with the memory loss. So why did everyone act as if they didn't know her? Surely if they knew Johnny, they'd know his wife.

Unless she'd been a terrible snob before her accident and that was why no one wanted to speak to her.

That possibility paralyzed her. Too embarrassed by what his answer might be, she didn't voice her fears and questions aloud. He deserved a wife who was held in the same esteem the townspeople had for him.

Johnny stopped to give a stranger directions to a local B and B. Trying to suppress her fears, Marla turned to look in the window of an art gallery. She was admiring a watercolor seascape when the reflection of a man and a woman caught her attention. He was tall and slender, the woman red-haired and petite, both of them curiously familiar. He bent to kiss her....

Jealously and anger whipped through Marla, and she closed her eyes against the sight, against the feeling of betrayal. Nausea rose in her throat. Her hand flew to her mouth, her head throbbed. Unsteady, she braced her other hand against the cold glass of the window. She forced herself to breathe slowly through her nose.

"Are you all right?" Johnny asked, taking her arm.

"Fine. A little dizzy is all." When she opened her eyes, the couple were strolling by, laughing and smiling. She turned to stare into their faces, but they didn't acknowledge either her or Johnny. She didn't know them, had never seen them before. Why on earth would she react so strongly to seeing them kiss?

"Maybe we should find someplace to sit down. You don't look good."

"No. I want to keep walking." Away from that couple. Away from whatever had triggered that terrible sense of betrayal. She hurried along the sidewalk, almost dragging Johnny with her, until she reached a shop displaying baby things. "Oh, let's go inside. Maybe we'll find something for Caitlin."

"Or Teresa, if Mama has her way."

She laughed, feeling lighthearted again. Thoughts of her baby did that to her. A bell chimed as they stepped through the open doorway.

"Hi, Chief Fuentes. Can I help you?" The store clerk appeared to be about eighteen, her blond hair tightly permed, her jaw working hard on a piece of gum.

"Ah, we'll just browse, if that's okay?"

"Sure. Whatever." She went back to reading an entertainment magazine, her jaw working double time.

Marla was tempted to buy almost everything she saw. A frilly dress in a six-month size, totally impractical but adorable. A musical mobile with fuzzy teddy bears. Deliciously soft blankets in rainbow colors.

In spite of all the things Rita had brought for the baby, Marla had an urge to buy something special for Caitlin...or Teresa, if Mama Fuentes had her way, she thought with a smile. Something to bring her home in from the hospital. Something brand-new that was all her own.

After searching every shelf, she found a delicate gown in a pale peach with a tiny bit of lace around the hem and on the sleeves.

"What do you think of this?" she asked Johnny, who'd been ever so patient waiting for her.

He shrugged. "It's pretty. I don't know much about babies."

"You will soon enough, Daddy," she teased.

The store clerk's head popped up from her magazine and she glanced from Marla to Johnny and back again.

Embarrassed color stained his cheeks. ''Why don't you go ahead and get it.''

Tickled that a macho man like Johnny would blush, Marla automatically reached for her purse and was drawn up short. She had no purse, no wallet. No credit cards or checkbook. She didn't even have any ID.

All of that had been lost along with her memory.

The void that was her past rushed up to slap her back to reality. She felt naked and vulnerable. She couldn't prove she was Marla Fuentes...or anyone else. As far as the clerk was concerned, she was a nobody. Strictly a cash-and-carry customer, and she didn't have any cash, either.

Approaching Johnny, she said softly, ''I don't have any money. Could you—''

''Oh, sure.'' He pulled out his wallet.

''I must have lost all my credit cards during the accident.''

''Yeah. I guess so.'' He laid his card on the counter and Marla handed the gown to the clerk.

''We probably ought to report them lost.''

''I'll take care of it.''

She hoped he would. Though she couldn't know for sure, she didn't imagine a police chief in a town the size of Mar del Oro had an unlimited budget. She'd hate for someone to find her cards and run up bills Johnny would be responsible for paying.

"Are you ready to call it a day?" he asked as they left the store.

"Gracious, no. Don't you know women like to shop till they drop? I'm not even close yet."

"Where's your all-time favorite place to shop?"

"That's easy. Harrods in London, or anywhere in New York." Halting suddenly in the flow of sidewalk traffic, she looked up at Johnny. In her mind's eye, she could actually see Harrods as well as the exclusive shops along Fifth Avenue. "How did I know that?"

He eased her out of the way of passing pedestrians. "You remembered something. The doctor said your memory would come back in bits and pieces."

She searched her mind for other clues to her past, for images of *people*. Nothing surfaced except a welling of panic. "Why shopping? Why not my mother? Or my high school prom?" Or my wedding day? she wanted to ask.

Did Johnny have enough money for her to shop in New York and London? She glanced down at the ring on her finger, the diamond glistening in the sunlight. Had she demanded that extravagance of him, been that selfish?

With his fingertips, he smoothed back an errant lock of hair from her face. "Knowing my sisters, I'd say shopping holds an importance of magnitude ten over a prom. It's getting the dress that counts, not the guy you're going with."

"Oh, you..." Instead of letting herself cry or asking the questions that were on the tip of her tongue, she laughed. "Are you saying I wouldn't have remembered you if you'd taken me to the prom?"

He hooked his arm through hers and started jaywalking across the street through the slow-moving traffic. "Of course you would. I'm truly memorable. Unfortunately, you weren't living in del Oro during my prom days."

"Oh? And just who had the honor of being your date?"

"You sure you want to know?"

"I promise not to be jealous."

He stopped in the middle of the street while a car passed. "Heather McQuire. An absolute babe. Every guy in school was green with envy."

In spite of her promise, Marla *was* jealous. "Where is she now?"

"Don't know. Last I heard, she was living in Stockton, had three kids and had put on a hundred pounds."

"You're putting *me* on."

"Nope. But it might be only seventy-five pounds."

She nudged him in the ribs with her elbow. This was a teasing side of Johnny she hadn't seen...or couldn't remember. And she loved it.

They arrived on the opposite sidewalk right in front of Miniature World with its Dream Man Collection banner pasted on the front window.

"Let's go inside," Marla urged. "Maybe I can find myself a dream man."

"You mean to tell me I'm not already your dream man?" He opened the door for her.

"Of course you are, Johnny. But a girl has to keep her options open." Though she doubted any woman could find a better candidate for dream man than her blue knight.

"That's just like a woman—always keeping a man guessing."

Inside the shop, arrays of lead soldiers in full battle regalia were on display. Every war imaginable was represented, from Napoleonic times to World War II, with opposing armies set to mow each other down. An adjacent glass cabinet featured pewter figures from Tolkien's *The Lord of the Rings,* gargoyles and dragons breathing fire.

Each of the miniatures was a true work of art, carefully crafted and painted in precise detail. Marla admired them all.

A tall woman with angular features appeared from the back of the store. "Hey, Johnny. Did you assign yourself to foot patrol this weekend?"

"Nope. We're playing tourist today."

The woman's interested gaze slid toward Marla. "Welcome to Mar del Oro."

"Thank you. Your merchandise is exquisite."

"We work hard to maintain our quality."

Both women waited for an introduction. Finally, Johnny took the hint. "Ah, Dora, this is Marla...my wife. Dora Pennington."

"Your...w-wife?" Dora stammered. "Well, gee, that's wonderful." She extended her hand and smiled warmly. "I'm really glad to meet you."

Marla responded in kind, but inside, she had another of those troubling, uneasy feelings. Why was it she'd never met Dora before? Nothing about Johnny's expression gave away the answer to that question.

A family of tourists arrived in the shop and Dora went to help them. Marla turned her attention back to the merchandise. Casually she asked, "Have you known Dora long?"

"We went to high school together. She was a couple of years behind me. Her dad owned the store then. She took over a few years ago after he had a heart attack."

Obviously, he knew Dora pretty well. Why hadn't she so much as met the woman?

In a display cabinet near the rear of the shop, Marla spotted a medieval knight mounted on a horse, and she smiled. No more than four inches tall, with helmet and breastplate painted blue, he held his lance at the ready, prepared to charge his opponent. At the end of the lance, a tiny bit of fabric dangled—his lady love's colors, Marla guessed. Amazingly, the bit of silk resembled the yellow polka-dot scarf she'd been wearing when Johnny had brought her to the hospital.

Carefully, she lifted the knight's helmet from his head. The noble warrior had dark hair, a square jaw and brown eyes so sympathetic his compassion reached out to Marla, embracing her in an instant.

"It's you," she whispered, awed.

"What is?"

"The blue knight." Tears pricked at the back of her eyes as she looked up at Johnny. "The artist could've been using you for a model."

He frowned. "I don't see any particular resemblance."

With her fingertips, she caressed his cheek, roughened with just a trace of dark whiskers. "I do. My own personal dream man, my blue knight in shining armor."

Chapter Five

He took her hand and pressed a kiss to her palm.
"Don't think of me like that, kitten. I'm just a man."

"A noble one."

"Not nearly noble enough." He wanted another
man's wife, and that wasn't honorable at all. "Did
you want to buy anything here? Or are you ready to
go?"

She glanced longingly at the four-inch-high miniature. "I'm ready."

When they reached the front counter, Dora was on
the phone, looking grim. "No, I understand, Janet,"
she said. "Those things happen and I'm so sorry for
you. I'll manage somehow. You take care of yourself,
you hear?"

She hung up with a sigh.

"Doesn't sound like good news," Johnny commented.

"It's not. The woman who works from home painting most of the miniatures we make in-house slipped
in the bathtub this morning and broke her wrist. She's
been at the hospital for hours getting X rays and a

cast on her arm. That'd be bad under any circumstances, but I've got a special order for a whole company of Union soldiers and the Confederates to match them that's due to be shipped next week. I don't know who on earth I'll find to paint them. Or how I'll ever find the time myself, but I guess I'll have to—''

"I could help," Marla said softly.

Both Johnny and Dora turned to her, and Marla felt a wave of self-consciousness heat her cheeks.

"You don't have to do that," Dora assured her. "I'm sure—"

"Really, I'd like to help. If I just sit around all day waiting for the baby to arrive, I'll be bored to tears." She rested her hand on her belly and smiled. "Of course, after she comes, I'll probably be busier than I'd really like and won't be getting enough sleep. But for the next couple of weeks..."

Dora sent Johnny a questioning look.

He shrugged. "It's fine by me if she wants to give it a shot."

"It's not exactly hard work," Dora admitted, smiling at Marla and looking relieved. "All you need is a steady hand and a good eye for detail. I'll pay you the same as I do Janet. You won't be getting rich, I'll promise you that."

"The money doesn't matter." Marla had the feeling there were a great many other things in life that were more important than being rich—being useful among them. And having friends. Johnny had such a wealth of caring friends and loving family members, Marla wanted to share in the richness of his life. And she couldn't understand why everyone she met seemed so startled to learn she was Johnny's wife.

Dora took them to the back room where there were worktables and rows of black rubber molds, each one marked with the soldier's army, his unit and his posture—parade rest, kneeling to fire or charging the enemy with bayonet at the ready. The whole process of creating a mold by first sculpting the figure in wax or clay fascinated Marla. Her fingers itched to create something herself, and she searched her memory to discover if she'd once tried her hand at being an artist.

As usual, nothing came to mind except the same blank wall. Had she no interests, no talents? How had she spent her days?

Johnny left to jog home and bring his car so they could more easily carry the four dozen miniatures back to the house. While he was gone, Dora gave Marla some painted soldiers to use as samples.

"You're sure you're all right with this?" Dora asked, lining up tiny bottles of acrylic paint for Marla to take along. "I don't want to impose on Johnny's friendship."

"You're not. Helping out was my idea." She fingered one of the brushes that had no more than three or four hairs, used for the most delicate painting. She wanted to ask Dora why she hadn't known her before, why they weren't already friends. But something held her back.

Perhaps she didn't want to face the truth of who she was, how lacking she'd been as a friend. Whatever the case, she vowed she'd do better. She wanted Johnny to be proud of her.

Two DAYS LATER, Marla sat at the kitchen table diligently painting a Union captain's half-inch sword a silver-gray. The sun streamed through the window, landing on the captain's blue-clad troops. The Confederate soldiers were still in the box waiting their turn to be properly garbed. Outside, the ocean's hum kept her company along with the cry of an occasional sea gull.

She heard Johnny's car pull up out front and checked her watch. The day had flown by so quickly she hadn't started dinner yet.

When he stepped into the house, her heart did a little stutter step. While men in military uniforms might be fine for some women, she'd choose a police chief dressed in blue any day of the week.

"Hi," she said, straightening and rubbing the small of her back.

Crossing the room, he gave the array of lead soldiers an approving look. "You're making good progress."

"As Dora suggested, it's not exactly rocket science, but I'm having a good time. If I get a little bored, I let my mind wander and give them names."

"Names?"

"And their own personal histories. Our brave captain here is Geoffrey Smothers of the Massachusetts First Infantry. Handsome fellow, don't you think?"

Amused, he shook his head. "I'd say you have a better imagination than I do."

"I can name you the battles he's fought in, if you'd like."

"Maybe later." He produced a small box about five inches square from behind his back and handed it to her. The gold-embossed label on the top read Dream Man Collection.

Excitement rippled through her and her gaze snapped up. "What's this?"

"For you. Open it and see for yourself." He looked as pleased as punch with himself, his slightly crooked smile like that of a mischievous boy.

She knew what was inside, and her fingers shook as she lifted the lid. A band squeezed tight around her chest. He'd known how much she'd admired the miniature at the store and had bought it for her.

The medieval knight mounted on a high-stepping horse rested on its side in molded plastic, his shield and armor a bright blue. Carefully, she lifted the figure and placed it on the table. Taking the lance with its tiny bit of polka-dot fabric, she slid it into the knight's hand, then placed his helmet on his head.

Her Johnny, her noble knight.

"You shouldn't have," she whispered, touched by his gesture more than she could express. When was the last time she'd received a gift? With her faulty memory, this was her first and her most cherished. She looked up at him with tears in her eyes. "Thank you."

He cleared his throat. "At least with that knight around, maybe you won't forget me."

Standing, she linked her arms around his neck. "I'll never forget you, Johnny. I promise."

She initiated the kiss, hungry for what they'd been denying themselves. With their unborn child between them, their embrace held a special intimacy, a closeness that only lovers could achieve. The warmth of his body, his maleness, protected Marla and their child, engulfed them both in a sea of comfort and security.

As his arms closed around her, Marla let her tongue explore the shape of his lips, teasing at the crease until he allowed her entry. He groaned and so did she. The taste of him was exquisitely male, sharp and fresh.

Her fingers combed through the thick hair at his nape; his hands closed over her hips, pulling her as close as her figure would allow.

With another murmur of pleasure, he became the aggressor. His tongue parried with hers. She responded, adjusting the angle of their lips, sucking in his flavor, savoring it. Her breathing became labored, her heartbeat accelerating.

"Marla..." he gasped, dragging in a deep breath and holding her tight.

"I know. We can't." But they must have been great together before her pregnancy had brought their love life to a halt—hot and wild and instantly eager. With a single kiss, he aroused her to a fevered pitch. Even at night when he simply held her, she teetered on the brink of sexual excitement. As far as Marla was concerned, the delivery of their child and her own rapid recovery couldn't happen fast enough.

She gave him a shaky smile. "I promise you, after the baby comes, you and I are going to lock ourselves in together for twenty-four hours straight and do this thing right."

"Promises, promises." He chuckled. "And just what do you propose we do about 2:00 a.m. feedings?"

"Oh, that." Laughing, she rested her head on his shoulder. Such a solid man and so constant with his friends and family. "We'll think of something," she said, knowing she was among the world's most fortunate women.

He took a step back. "So where are you going to put your shining knight?"

She glanced around. "Right on the mantel next to all your triathlon trophies, of course."

"Hmm, does that make me a trophy husband?"

"The very best kind." She grinned and gave him another quick kiss.

After she placed the knight on the mantel, she stepped back to admire him one more time. What gifts, she wondered, had she given her husband?

"Johnny, when is our anniversary?"

"Anniversary?" He coughed. "Uh, you know men are notoriously bad at remembering things like that."

"Well, how long have we been married?"

Johnny turned hastily and went into the kitchen. He opened the refrigerator, pulled out a canned drink and popped the top. "It seems like only yesterday, kitten."

She frowned. Was he being intentionally evasive? Or didn't their wedding date mean anything to him? Twisting her ring, she closed her eyes and tried to picture herself in a wedding gown. An image actually formed—a long gown with a low-cut bodice, a strand of pearls and a veil hiding the bride's face. She searched her memory for a picture of the groom, of Johnny in a dark tux looking so handsome he'd take her breath away.

She sighed and opened her eyes when the memory failed to materialize. "I wish I could remember the details, but the harder I try—"

"The doctor said to let the memories come naturally and not to force yourself."

"Which is why you're not filling in the blanks for me?"

"The doctor thought that would be best."

Gritting her teeth, she thought, *To hell with the doctor!* "You sure you wouldn't like to share the details of our honeymoon? That's something a woman really ought to remember."

His dark-eyed gaze swept over her slowly, sensuously lingering on her breasts and the fullness of her belly. "I'll tell you this, kitten. You were the greatest, absolutely the greatest."

Warmth flooded her body. The sexual tension she'd been feeling wasn't one-sided. He felt it, too. She rejoiced in that knowledge. Even if she never got answers to her other questions, he'd told her what she wanted to know about the most important one.

He did care for her; he hadn't been forced by her pregnancy into an unwanted marriage.

THAT NIGHT, IT WAS ALL Johnny could do not to ignore the doctor's advice—and his own good sense—and make love with Marla. Her kisses had aroused him as no other woman's had. The scent of her, the feel of her breasts pressing against him, the swell of her belly, all gave him ideas he shouldn't be entertaining. Yet he couldn't stop the images that floated through his mind both day and night.

Marla in his arms, kissing her more fully, kissing her everywhere, filling her with his need.

She belonged to someone else.

And she was beginning to ask questions he couldn't answer. *Vague* didn't begin to describe his responses. *Lies* was closer to the truth, and it grated on him that he wasn't able to be open and honest with Marla. She deserved better.

By morning, he was as snarly as a grizzly just coming out of hibernation and as frustrated as hell. He was going to get the station's Polaroid camera, take her picture and have it broadcast over every TV station in California and beyond. Someone had to know Marla; someone had to be looking for her.

And the most likely someone of all had to be her husband. Though why the hell he hadn't filed a missing-person report was beyond Johnny. If she'd been his wife, he would have moved heaven and earth to find her again.

He stormed into the police station and had barely stepped inside his office when Lynel showed up.

"I think I have a lead on your mystery woman, Chief." He handed Johnny an all-points bulletin that had come off the wires.

Dread tightened in Johnny's gut. The grainy black-and-white photo taken from a surveillance camera could be of Marla. She had long hair, described as dark blond, but her features didn't look as symmetrical as Marla's or as carefully sculpted. She was thirty-four years old; Marla seemed younger, more innocent. The height and weight were right on target though there was no mention of her being pregnant.

But the worst was that this stranger in the photo was wanted in connection with a series of armed robberies at convenience stores around Los Angeles. Her partner had been apprehended and named his accomplice, telling the local authorities Stephanne Turick had fled the area about a week ago—just about the time Marla had appeared in Mar del Oro with amnesia.

"Damn," Johnny muttered, spearing his fingers through his hair.

He couldn't ignore this lead. Nor could he believe the woman he knew as Marla, the woman he'd held in his arms and wanted to make love with, would rob convenience stores at gunpoint. But a lot of men made fools of themselves over a woman. He wouldn't be the first—or the last.

''Get me the Polaroid from booking,'' he ordered.

''You think it's her, the woman you found on the beach?''

He hoped not. God, he hoped not. ''I'll take a couple of pictures and we'll send them down to L.A., see if they can ID her.''

''Patty says she's living with you.''

''Yeah. It's a temporary arrangement.'' Until he found her husband, she got her memory back—or he locked her up in jail. Hell of a choice!

SHE'D FORGOTTEN TO TELL Johnny she had an appointment with the obstetrician that morning, the one who'd seen her while she'd been in the hospital. He would have driven her into town, she was sure. But she hated to bother him by calling the office, a number he'd made sure she had in case of an emergency. And she did, after all, need to get some exercise. Hunching over a table painting four-inch-high figures all day wasn't exactly conducive to deep breathing.

Walking up the last hill to the hospital and adjacent medical building was, however. She was huffing by the time she reached the doctor's office.

''Do you have your insurance card with you?'' asked the receptionist, a young woman with wide eyes and dark hair that dipped into a deep widow's peak.

''No, I lost it.'' Another bit of her past that had vanished in the accident. ''If it helps, Johnny Fuentes is my husband.''

''The chief of police?''

"Yes." Marla basked in the reflected pride that everyone in town knew her Johnny. *So why didn't they know her?* Had he kept her hidden in a closet the whole time they'd been married? Or had she been such a snob she hadn't come out of the house?

"Really? Well, I guess we can trust him, can't we?" With a smile, the receptionist handed Marla a clipboard with a form for new patients to complete. "Just bring in your new card when you get it."

"Thanks. I will."

Turning, she picked a seat in the crowded waiting room next to a woman about her own age. She was jiggling a baby on her lap, cooing motherly nonsense words to the child.

"She's adorable," Marla said. "How old is she?"

"About three months."

Marla studied the child's tiny features and her cap of dark hair that was so different from her mother's much fairer coloring. "Is she in for a checkup?"

"Actually, no. I am. I'm pregnant."

Marla very nearly gasped aloud. "Already? I mean, I didn't think a woman could get pregnant so soon after... Not that it's any of my business, but whew!"

The young woman laughed. "It is a frightening prospect to have two babies so close together. But in this case, I didn't do all the work myself. Betina is adopted."

Marla went very still. Deep in her chest, a feeling of emptiness arose. "Sometimes it's hard to be adopted," she said thoughtfully, her hand resting on her belly. "You can feel like you don't be-long…anywhere."

"I hope Bets never feels like that. My husband and I both love her very much."

Marla blinked, realizing she hadn't been thinking about the woman and baby next to her but of someone else. "I'm sorry. That was a foolish thing to say. I don't even know why I said it. I think it's wonderful when couples adopt babies who were unwanted—"

"Bets's mother and father wanted her very much, but they both died as a result of a car accident. Be-tina's mother wanted my husband to raise her and you can be sure she'll always know how much her parents loved her."

Embarrassment heated Marla's cheeks. "This ap-pears to be my day for sticking my foot in my mouth. Which is a really hard trick to do, given my fat belly. I'm truly sorry for what I said. I don't know what I was thinking about."

"Don't worry about it." The woman bounced the smiling baby on her knees again. "By the way, I'm Ann Forrester Drummond. Did I hear you say you're Johnny Fuentes's wife?"

"Yes. Do you know him?"

"Oh, sure. We don't actually socialize much—we just see each other around town—but we did go to school together. He also managed to lock me up in his jail once, too."

"You?" Ann didn't exactly look like the criminal type. Impeccably groomed with long blond hair and intelligent green eyes, she looked more like a conservative schoolteacher dressed in designer jeans and a cotton blouse.

"Fortunately, it was a mistake. But it's not an experience I'd want to repeat any time soon."

The thought of being locked behind bars even briefly raised gooseflesh down Marla's spine. "I can certainly understand your reluctance. I'd probably be screaming with claustrophobia in about two seconds flat."

"The humiliation was what got me," Ann admitted with a wry smile.

Marla agreed that would be a problem, too, particularly since she was the police chief's wife. But being locked in a cell? She shuddered again. For some reason she couldn't remember—or didn't care to—she hated small, enclosed places. Perhaps she had at least one memory that was better forgotten.

The nurse called Ann into the examining room, and Marla got to work completing the patient information form. She'd certainly had an odd reaction to Ann's mention of adoption, as if she found the process distasteful. That wasn't how she felt. Not at all. But unexpectedly, at some gut level, she'd responded negatively.

Just another one of those memory glitches, she supposed, in the same way she couldn't for the life of her recall if she'd had chicken pox or mumps. To her surprise, however, she'd automatically written September 12 as her birth date and discovered she would soon turn thirty.

She let that small puzzle piece slide into place in

her brain. Perhaps it would nudge other bits of her memory out into the light of day—like why adoption had an unhappy connotation for her and why she felt she was claustrophobic.

As she completed the form and returned it to the receptionist, she had another troubling thought. Why didn't the doctor already have her patient history on file?

JOHNNY WAS FRANTIC.

He'd come home expecting to find Marla at work painting her miniatures. He'd planned to take her picture, act as if he was trying out a new camera that the department had purchased so she wouldn't know what he was up to. But she wasn't there.

For a terrible moment, he was afraid she'd gotten wind of the all-points bulletin regarding Stephanne Turick and she'd fled before being arrested. But that wasn't possible. There was no way she could have known.

He stepped out onto the back deck, thinking she might have taken a walk along the beach. A steady, salt-flavored breeze caught his hair and blew it across his forehead. As far as he could see, only one family was strolling along the sand at the waterline and another couple was sunbathing in a cluster of rocks near the cliff walkway that provided public access to the beach.

No Marla.

Dammit all! She wasn't a criminal. He would have sensed it, would have seen the guilt in her eyes.

But he had to pursue the possibility.

He marched back inside, snatched the camera from the table where he'd left it and headed out to his car. That's when he spotted her halfway down the block. Relief surged through him along with a sense of satisfaction. She was coming home to him.

But she wasn't coming home alone, he realized an instant later. He squinted. A dog? Where the hell...?

She waved, smiling. "Hi, honey. Look what I found."

Little more than a puppy, the dog was a mixed-breed, short-haired mutt with floppy black ears, big feet, and a rib cage with every bone visible.

"Where'd you find him?" Johnny asked.

"Right by the freeway off-ramp. He was so scared, Johnny, with all those cars racing by. And you can see how hungry he is. He probably hasn't eaten in a week or more."

"So you brought him home."

"Well, he sort of followed me."

"Uh-huh. That wouldn't have anything to do with the groceries you're carrying, would it?" he asked, eyeing the plastic bag in her hand.

"I stopped at the grocery store after my doctor's appointment to pick up a few things, and I did happen to have a can of chicken with me. One of those easy-opening cans with a pop-top." She grinned. "I was going to make a chicken salad tonight."

A doctor's appointment. Purely innocent. He should have known. "I gather the dog enjoyed our dinner."

"Only the main ingredient. I'll find something else for us."

He looked down at the dog, who'd planted himself almost on top of Marla's foot and was gazing up at her expectantly. His tail twitched from side to side; he licked his chops.

"I suppose we could take him to the pound," Marla said softly, a plea to do just the opposite in her sea-green eyes.

Yep, Johnny had always been a sucker for the underdog—or a compassionate woman. "Of course, if we did that, you'd never forgive me."

"What a silly thing to say, Johnny. Of course I'd forgive you." She grinned, and her eyes sparkled in the lighthearted way that he liked to see and was all too rare. "In about a hundred years."

With a shake of his head, he said, "Come on, let's see what else we can find for that mutt to eat. Given the size of his feet, I have the uncomfortable feeling it's going to take a lot to fill him up."

Marla slipped her arm around Johnny's waist and somehow he didn't mind that she'd brought home a stray pooch that was going to cost him a bundle in dog food and vet bills.

"I've come up with the perfect name for him."

"Why am I not surprised? You've named all those lead soldiers in the house."

"Beauregard."

"Huh? Isn't that a little pretentious for a mutt?"

"All the more reason why he needs an aristocratic name since his ancestry is definitely in question."

They laughed and went inside together. Johnny used the dog as an excuse to take some pictures, always including her in the scene. Her smile, with her straight white teeth and happy glint in her eyes, warmed his heart even as he worried that the LAPD might ID her as a criminal.

The last photo he set aside. He'd keep that one for himself—so he wouldn't forget her. Not that he'd need a picture for that. She'd already insinuated herself in his heart. It was going to hurt like hell when she left, whatever the reason.

"I guess we should take Beau to the vet to get a checkup and be sure he has his shots," Marla said while peering into the hopelessly empty freezer for something to defrost for dinner to go with the salad makings she'd bought at the store.

"I could probably take him Saturday." He sorted through the Polaroid shots as if they were a deck of cards—all the queen of hearts and her court jester. "Oh, no, I can't. That's the Teen Day baseball game. I'll have to find another day."

"Teen Day?" she asked over her shoulder.

"Yeah, once a year, police and fire challenge the local teenagers to a game of softball. It's a fund-raiser for an after-school sports program the city puts on. There's a picnic, too. The whole town turns out."

"Sounds like fun."

"You like picnics and baseball?" He knew so little about her and she knew so little about herself.

"Picnics I can handle. But I don't think you want me on your baseball team. Beyond the fact that I've never been particularly athletic, I don't think I'd be able to waddle around the bases fast enough even if I somehow managed to hit the ball.''

''You're not athletic?''

She spread her arms and grinned, a smile that made her eyes sparkle. ''Look at me. With this figure, do you think I ought to take up the discus or the hundred-yard barrel roll?''

''How 'bout I sign you up to be a fan?''

''Absolutely. If I get to root for you.''

How did she know she wasn't athletic? he wondered. And had she gained other insights about herself since her accident and subsequent amnesia? Including a criminal past? he couldn't help thinking with a sense of unease.

For now, he'd have to return to the station and send the photos of her off to Los Angeles. It would be a few days before he got an answer back.

He hoped it was the answer he wanted.

Meanwhile, he had a serious problem. If he was going to introduce her at the picnic as his wife, a lot of eyebrows were likely to be raised. Folks were certain to ask him questions he couldn't answer.

And until Marla had her baby, Johnny had to keep up the charade of being her husband. Not that the role wasn't becoming more comfortable with each passing day.

Too comfortable, he chided himself as she bent over to retrieve a pot from the cupboard. He liked having Marla in his house…and in his bed.

Chapter Six

Marla reached for Johnny's hand to steady her past an outcropping of uneven rocks on the beach. She often found herself making excuses to touch him, to link her fingers with his stronger ones.

In this case, the advantage of taking her daily walk in the evening was that Johnny could join her. After just one day, Beau had become a member of the family and now joined them on their walks. She laughed as the puppy dashed toward the waves, trying to snap up the froth that curled along the shoreline.

"You have a wonderful laugh," Johnny said.

She turned, startled by his remark. "Why, thank you." Barefoot, he was wearing shorts and a white T-shirt that pulled tautly across his chest, revealing the outline of muscles and sinew. His legs were those of a runner, lean and strong and roughened by a light furring of dark hair. Her palms itched to renew her memories of that forgotten territory.

"You should laugh more often."

Pausing a moment, she tried to recall the last time

she'd laughed out loud. Not since her accident, she realized. But hadn't she enjoyed life before that?

"Maybe you should have gotten me a puppy as a wedding present," she said, only half-teasing.

"Maybe you're right."

He seemed so serious, so intense, she didn't know quite how to respond. "Did you have pets when you were young?"

"Not likely. Though most of the farms had a dog or two hanging around. Cats, too."

"You lived on a farm?" How terrible she'd forgotten as much about her husband's life as she had about her own. "I'm sorry I can't remember—"

"It's not important. It was a long time ago anyway."

To Marla, his answer sounded evasive, but she let it slide as Beau dragged an ungainly piece of seaweed away from the water's edge and proudly dropped it at her feet. "Good boy," she said, rewarding the dog with a pat on his head.

"Don't encourage him. Next thing you know, he'll be hauling every bit of junk he can find up to the house."

She laughed again. "Maybe he'll find us some buried treasure. We could always use a few gold doubloons."

"That's true enough."

The breeze billowed her oversize blouse and caught her hair, blowing it across her face. She shoved the wayward strands back behind her ear. Offshore, a fog bank was building. But here the sun was still bright enough to make her squint. Shivering slightly at the misty memory of being caught in dense fog, she vowed they'd return to the house before the cloud crept on shore.

Wanting to lighten the mood again, she asked, "If Beau really managed to find us a fortune in doubloons, or we won the lottery—" she grinned at him "—what would you do with the money?"

"My tastes are pretty simple, Marla. I doubt if having a lot of money would change my life very much."

"Surely you want something you don't have now. What do you dream about?"

His low, raspy chuckle skittered down her spine. "I dream about you, kitten. Naked and sexy as hell. That's the kind of dream guys have."

A flush of pleasure stole up her cheeks. "Besides that, I mean."

He slid his arm around her waist. "No, you tell me. Would you buy a bigger, fancier house if you had all the money you wanted?"

"Not if it meant giving up the view from the kitchen window. That's worth a fortune."

"So what would you spend the money on?"

She frowned, trying to think what her forgotten dreams might be. "I'd paint the house. It definitely needs it."

"I've been planning to get around to that. What else?"

"We could hang some nice paintings on the walls. You know, originals like that watercolor I saw in town the other day."

"I could probably afford one or two right now, not that I'd know what to buy."

"I would. I'm pretty good at identifying..." Her voice trailed off and her forehead furrowed again. "Do I know something about art? I mean, really?"

"A helluva lot more than I do."

The image of an art gallery popped into her mind. Not a small gallery like those in Mar del Oro but something much larger and classical in style with the masters on display—Rembrandt, Van Gogh, Goya. She'd been there, studied the paintings. Around her, she heard a low murmur of voices, almost like the sea rolling against the shore, but she couldn't make out the words. Couldn't understand what they were saying.

Dizzy, she closed her eyes.

"Marla, are you all right?"

She blinked. The image had vanished. "Yes, I'm—I'm fine. I was just thinking.... If I had the money, I'd like to go to art museums. Maybe in France or Italy." Or perhaps she'd already been there and couldn't quite remember the trip.

"Sure. As soon as Beau drags home a trunk full of gold coins, I'll make the reservations."

Turning, she looped her arms around his neck. "You're such a good man, Johnny Fuentes. And I'm so lucky to have found you. Maybe we will find the pot of gold somewhere. But if we don't, it doesn't matter. Not as long as we have each other."

Standing on tiptoe, she kissed him. She'd only meant it to be a swift kiss, but he deepened it of his own accord even though she'd caught him off guard. She plowed her fingers through the hair at his nape as his tongue toyed with hers. The salt-flavored air mixed with his own special taste, and she relished the essence of a man and the sea.

They didn't do enough kissing, she thought distractedly. It was something she really liked; at least with Johnny that was true. His combination of strength and gentleness undid her, and she didn't think it was only a result of her raging hormones. Unfortunately, her advanced pregnancy restricted their ability to fully make love together. But there were alternatives, ways a couple could enjoy—

A sudden shower of water drenched them. They jumped apart as though they'd been shot.

"Beau!" Johnny bellowed. "Quit that!"

Having shaken himself mostly dry, the puppy hit the ground with his tummy, groveling on the sand.

In spite of herself, Marla laughed breathlessly. "He certainly gives new meaning to taking a cold shower, doesn't he?"

Johnny scowled. "Smart dog," he grumbled.

THAT NIGHT IN BED when Marla tucked her sweet little rear end against Johnny's groin, he wondered where the hell he'd find the self-control not to take advantage of the situation.

Sure, he'd walked on the beach with a lot of women. He'd kissed a few, too. But never had a woman's laughter so ignited his imagination. If that dumb dog hadn't sprayed them with icy cold water when he did, chances were good that Johnny would have had Marla down on the sand, making love to her within milliseconds. She'd made him that hot with her kisses.

Not a good plan.

Even so, with his arm draped over her midsection now, he reveled in the brush of her breasts against his forearm, the swell of her belly ripe with child. Pregnant women weren't supposed to be that sexy. But he wanted her.

And she belonged to someone else.

Who? he wondered for about the ten thousandth time. It made no sense that someone hadn't filed a missing-person report on her. A woman this sweet and caring had to have a hundred friends who'd be checking on her, wondering where she was. And a husband who ought to be frantic with worry.

Unless he was dead. Maybe in the same car accident that injured Marla.

Briefly, Johnny considered what would happen if she was indeed a widow. It still wouldn't change anything between them. They probably came from two totally different worlds.

What the hell did he know about art? Except for a gallery in del Oro where he'd investigated a break-in, he'd never set foot in anything resembling an art museum. He'd be like the proverbial bull in a china shop, and a dumb one at that.

THE NEXT MORNING, Marla came down the hallway from the kitchen just as Johnny was exiting the bathroom. She stopped dead in her tracks.

Bare-chested, with only a towel around his waist, the man was gorgeous, like a woman's fantasy appearing out of a steamy mist.

A faint trail of dark hair circled his nipples and arrowed south to points a wife should know intimately, details she had forgotten. His physique was solid, like the athlete he was, but his muscles didn't bulge in an intimidating way. He was simply masculine perfection.

Her mouth went dry. *Hormones,* she thought again.

With an effort, she dragged her gaze up to his, cleared her throat before she spoke, her thoughts lingering on what it would be like to rediscover each intriguing plane and valley of Johnny's powerful physique.

"I thought I'd do eggs for you this morning. But I can't remember how you like them."

"I usually just have cereal."

"I guess I'm into the nesting thing. Pregnant women do that, I'm told. Besides, you've done so much for me lately, I want to reciprocate." Actually, she wanted to do far more than make him breakfast. But the doctor had told her they shouldn't. And Johnny hadn't pressed to overturn the medical edict.

"Sunny-side up is good."

"Great. I'll try not to break the yolks."

Gripping the towel around his waist, Johnny waited for Marla to turn and go back to the kitchen. Her eager, lighthearted smile and the way she'd raked him over with her gaze had done something to Johnny's insides, not to mention his body's other, more carnal response. Her easy presence, the way she was trying to be so domestic, made him feel too much like they really were married.

He knew darn well if they truly were married, he'd be late to work this morning. His willingness to accept the invitation in her eyes would have been too potent to resist.

Upset with his inability to control his reactions, he went into the bedroom and pulled a clean uniform shirt out of the closet. He was spending too much time with her—both in and out of bed—that's what was wrong. His libido was working overtime. If he had any smarts, he'd use the cot at the office and sleep there tonight.

But given her advanced pregnancy, he couldn't very well leave her alone all day and all night. She could go into labor any time now. She didn't have anyone else except him to watch out for her.

He gritted his teeth. They'd never said anything about this kind of an assignment in the police academy. It had to fall into the advanced class for ''undercover'' work.

AFTER JOHNNY WENT TO WORK and Marla had cleaned up the kitchen, she sat down to continue painting the Civil War figures. One by one she dabbed tiny spots of black on the blue coats for buttons, using one of the fine brushes Dora had given her. Beau was curled at her feet, napping. The quiet house was like a safe haven, a peaceful place to escape from—

Her thoughts halted abruptly on the word *escape*.

Escape from what?

She would never want to leave Johnny. Yet she had the feeling that she'd once fled from somewhere…or had wanted to.

The image of a sprawling Tudor house with a circular driveway mocked her again, and an aura of loneliness surrounded her like trees encroaching on sunlight. Pain lanced her temple.

Blinking the sense of foreboding away, she stood, her muscles stiff from sitting so long. "I'm not going to think about that place," she said aloud.

Beau whined in response.

"You're right. What we need to do is go outside," she said to the dog. "It's too nice a day to be stuck inside."

The early-morning clouds had rolled back out to sea, and the sun was high in a clear blue sky. Standing on the front porch, she inhaled the salt-tinged air as though the freshness would drive the shadows of the past from her mind. As usual, the street was quiet, the neighbors presumably at work at this hour. Marla wondered what they were like and if she had met any of them.

She watched Beau circle the yard, sniffing every bush and shrub to determine what other creatures had visited his territory overnight, then mark it all once more with his own scent.

The yard really did need some work, she thought

idly as Beau continued his explorations. If she thought she could get back up again on her own, she'd consider pulling a few weeds. But her distended abdomen severely limited her mobility. She chuckled at the thought of Johnny coming home for dinner to find her stranded on the front lawn, as immobile as a turtle on its back.

Beau barked and raced off toward their neighbor's yard.

"Beau! Come back here! Beau!" He didn't so much as hesitate as he raced toward the letter carrier. Marla trotted after the dog as fast as she could manage.

The mailman halted in his tracks. Fortunately, Beau's tail was wagging with friendship. If he'd ever had obedience training—which seemed unlikely— he'd forgotten everything he'd learned.

"He's harmless," Marla called.

"Yes, ma'am, but these young'uns shore are excitable."

"He is that." She grabbed Beau's collar on his third trip around the mailman. "My husband's going to take him to the vet for shots this afternoon or tomorrow. Maybe I ought to ask him to get some tranquilizers, too."

"Shame to waste all that energy, isn't it? If'n you could harness it, you could go into competition with the power company."

She laughed. "What a good idea."

The man produced a handful of mail. "Here you

go, Mrs., uh…'' He glanced at the top letter. "Fuentes. You have yourself a nice day, you hear?''

"Yes, I will. Thank you. You, too.'' She smiled as he walked down the sidewalk. *Mrs. Fuentes.* At least the mailman knew who she was. That was reassuring.

In her belly, the baby gave her a kick, almost like an exclamation mark, insisting she liked being a Fuentes, too.

She dragged Beau back inside. Clearly, without a fenced yard, she'd have to ask Johnny to fix a run of some sort for the dog so he could be outside on his own.

Sorting through the mail, she found one envelope addressed to Mr. and Mrs. John Fuentes. After a moment's hesitation, which she couldn't quite explain, she opened it. The flyer inside advertised Charm Your Man apparel in San Luis Obispo, the garments so skimpy and see-through that Marla felt a blush creep up her neck. Her figure wouldn't do the teddies justice at the moment, but later, after the baby arrived, she just might visit the store.

She grinned. Wouldn't Johnny just love to see her in one of those outfits. She could imagine his eyes darkening to nearly black, the hard press of his arousal against her as he took her in his arms, pulling her close. The feel of his mouth on her. Everywhere.

Her breathing accelerated as the images proceeded to take on ever more intimacy. He was a passionate man. Even if she couldn't remember the particulars, she sensed that in every bone in her body every time he touched her. Kissed her. Making love with Johnny would be an experience no woman could ever forget.

Yet she had.

Groaning aloud, she went to the mantel and caressed the miniature knight with her fingertip.

"Help me remember," she whispered in a desperate plea, tears pooling in her eyes.

You're nothing but an iceberg in bed.

She started at the voice she heard inside her head. Where had that accusation come from?

Chapter Seven

Dolores Fuentes waved from the bleachers on the first-base side of the baseball diamond. "How's my baby Teresa doing?"

"She's doing fine, Mama," Johnny responded, ushering Marla toward the section where his family was seated.

Beau tugged on his leash, determined to sniff every new smell in the entire park. It was all Marla could do to keep from getting herself or someone else tangled in the lead. Evidently, she'd forgotten—or had never known—how much mischief puppies could get into or how much energy they had. At least Beau was housebroken. Unfortunately, Johnny's slippers appeared to be his favorite snack.

"Your mother is certainly determined the baby will be named Teresa," Marla said quietly. Although she'd been thinking Terri Fuentes had a nice ring to it, she wasn't quite ready to give up on Caitlin yet. She seemed to have an emotional attachment to the name though she couldn't remember why. It felt important to her, perhaps as a symbol for something positive in her forgotten past.

"Ignore her. She doesn't get a vote."

With Johnny's help, Marla climbed over the first row of benches to sit on the second tier for a better view of the field. "How about you? What name do you like best?"

He glanced at her with an unreadable look in his eyes. "I'll go along with whatever you decide."

Before Marla could suggest they ought to make the decision together, a boy about ten with Johnny's dark good looks scrambled down the bleachers from where Dolores was sitting. Two smaller versions from the same family tree followed close on his heels, the younger a girl. There was no sign of Rita, but Marla had no doubt who the children's mother would be.

"Hey, Uncle Johnny, you got a dog."

"Now my Juan really is a family man." Mama laughed. "A wife and a puppy, *sí?* That is good. And soon you'll be a daddy."

The children gathered around an ecstatic Beau, petting him and getting happy licks in return. The dog's tail was a blur, he was wagging it so fast and joyously. Marla smiled. Every child should have a dog. Her baby would.

Johnny leaned toward her. "I've gotta go take some warm-up tosses with the team. Will you be all right here?"

"Of course. And Beau's in seventh heaven with all this attention."

"This is Robbie, Nick and Michele," he said, naming the children in the order of their ages. "You kids behave yourselves, okay? Don't drive Marla crazy."

She took his hand and squeezed it. "I'll be fine. You just be sure to hit a home run or do something spectacular so I can cheer for you."

"I'll do my best." He smiled at her and ruffled Nick's hair in an easy gesture of affection. "The darn kids usually beat the socks off us old guys, though."

She watched him walk toward the dugout, admiring his buns in a pair of snug-fitting jeans, then turned to discover that Johnny's mother had moved down to join her.

"So tell me, how are you and my Johnny getting along?"

"Fine. He's a wonderful man."

She patted Marla's knee. "That's good. You're a pretty girl. You can make him happy."

Mama's comments seemed oddly out of place. Assuming Marla and Johnny had been married at least a year, which Marla guessed had to be the case since she was nearly nine months pregnant, why was Dolores belatedly giving her approval to their marriage? Had she originally harbored doubts about Johnny's choice of a wife? If so, why?

She glanced around the field looking for Johnny. She spotted him near first base talking to a woman. Her breath caught on a surge of jealousy. The redhead had a perfect figure, a slender waist and generous breasts. Compared to Marla and her present physique, she looked like a candidate for the Miss America crown.

Valiantly, Marla tried to tamp down her jealousy. Johnny was simply talking to a friend. He knew everyone in town. He would not betray her.

But another man had.

Bile rose in her throat and images sped through her mind like a videotape on fast forward. A woman with red hair, a tall man with brown hair whose face she couldn't distinguish. Their ghoulish laughter ringing in her ears, mocking her. A cheat, a swindler.

Then the image went black and dizziness spun through her.

"*Hija,* daughter, are you all right?" Johnny's mother asked.

Marla rubbed her forehead, the trace of the swelling still there where she'd hit her head, a dull ache lingering. But the pain in her chest was far more enduring, as though her heart had once been shattered and the scars had never healed.

Mama gently rubbed the small of Marla's back. "Is it the baby? Are you feeling something?"

"No, nothing like that." She tried to shake off the feeling of loss and betrayal, looking again for Johnny. This time, he was on second base fielding grounders a man at home base was hitting to him.

Her Johnny would not betray her, not her noble blue knight.

A GROUND BALL ROCKETED toward Johnny, and he made a dive for it, snaring it in time to toss it underhanded to the first baseman for an out. The crowd in the first-base bleachers cheered, the opposing fans groaned, and Johnny felt a whole bunch of muscles yelp that he hadn't used in a long time. Playing softball was a lot different than running and biking.

Trying not to wince, he got to his feet and grinned toward the bleachers. Marla smiled back at him, making the aches he would no doubt suffer later worth the effort. With her in the stands, he was having trouble concentrating. Not only did he want to show off for her, he wanted to do things with her he didn't have the right to be thinking about.

The next batter hit a pop-up for the third out, leaving the score seven to five for the kids in the fifth inning. Johnny jogged to the dugout.

"Hey, Chief." Lynel was standing on the bleacher side of the dugout fence. "The answer came in from L.A. that you were looking for."

"Yeah?" He slid a glance toward Marla, who was engrossed in a conversation with his three-year-old niece, their heads close together. Marla obviously had buckets full of patience and motherly instincts, but that didn't necessarily mean she wasn't in some kind of trouble. Yet she hadn't so much as flinched when he'd asked her if she knew anyone named Stephanne Turick, the suspect in the L.A. armed robbery. If Marla was a liar, she was a damn good one.

"No ID. Your friend isn't the suspect they're looking for."

Thank God! He exhaled the breath he'd been holding, his faith in his ability to judge others restored once again. "Thanks for letting me know."

"I figured you'd be anxious to hear, her living with you and all."

Lynel was right. He felt as if a weight had been lifted off his chest. But it still left him with the same old questions. Who was she? And where was her husband?

The hell of it was, everybody in town had heard Marla was his wife—including Tina from the coffee shop, who'd waylaid him before the game started. The situation was difficult to explain. Tina didn't have a lot of interest in the details and her temper had flared. She had stalked off in a huff. Johnny couldn't blame her. The situation and the possessive way he felt about Marla confused him, too.

But someone was likely to spill the beans soon and Marla would know the truth. They'd never been husband and wife. He'd lied to her. He'd led her on.

Admittedly, bringing her to the ball game was risky business. But dammit, he liked having her around. With luck, Mama and Rita would shield her from hearing the truth. The doctor didn't want her upset. As far as Johnny was concerned, that was a good enough reason to keep up his charade.

As he took his turn at bat, he glanced toward the stands. Rita, her kids and Beau were there, but Marla was gone. The third strike caught him looking the wrong direction.

Darn it all. Like an adolescent, he'd wanted to impress Marla with a big hit.

MARLA STEPPED INTO the snack shack through the open back door. The close quarters smelled like hot dogs and mustard, and two large trash containers were filled with ice and canned drinks.

"Rita sent me as her replacement. She's taking a break with her kids."

"Great. Pull up a pair of tongs and we'll let you handle the hot dogs."

Delighted to finally recognize someone in town she knew, Marla said, "Oh, hi, Ann, Rita didn't say you were—''

"Oh, I'm not Ann. I'm Jodie Sutherland, her sister."

The second woman in the shack pulled out a case of pop from under the counter. "I'm here, too."

Marla did a double take. "Twins?" Physically, the two were perfectly identical, although Jodie wore her hair in a long, blond braid down the middle of her back. They were dressed differently, too, Ann wearing neatly creased slacks with a cotton blouse and Jodie in sandals, an ankle-length dress and long loops of beads around her neck.

"Pretty scary that there are two of us, isn't it?" Jodie said with a laugh.

"Twice the trouble," Ann agreed.

Marla slipped next to them beside the hot dog roaster. "I think it's great. I used to envy girls who were close to their sisters."

"I did, too," Ann said. "I hated being an only child."

Marla looked at them blankly.

"We're confusing the poor woman," Jodie said,

making change for a customer. "Ann and I didn't know each other existed until a couple of months ago."

"We were adopted at birth by different families who weren't told we were twins."

Emotion tightened Marla's throat. She tried to control her inexplicable reaction to the subject of adoption, searching her faulty memory for a clue. She got a mental image of a child—a little girl who looked suspiciously like herself—and her stern-faced parents. *You don't belong.* And then the door into her mind slammed shut as if this was a scene Marla didn't want to examine too closely.

"And then Ann got arrested for a couple of bad checks I wrote."

"Which landed me in a jail cell, I might add."

"So she tracked me down and now we're best buddies," Jodie concluded.

"What a wonderful story," Marla said, her voice hoarse with the lump in her throat.

"We think so."

Ann gave Jodie a quick hug that filled Marla with envy. Instinctively, she knew she'd never had a sister. And she doubted she'd had a brother, either. She'd been alone, and lonely in a place where she didn't feel she belonged. A place where she'd wanted to be someone else.

Had she been unloved? Or unlovable? The possible answer filled her with dread.

Yet if she were so unlovable, why had Johnny married her? Had her pregnancy forced him to do the right thing? Was that why his mother had originally been hesitant about their marriage?

Her chin quivered. Dear God, she didn't want to be unlovable.

Jodie touched her shoulder sympathetically. "What's wrong, honey?"

She hesitated, afraid to voice her fears. "I think I may be adopted, too."

"You don't know for sure?"

"I had an accident. I can't remember...." So much of her past was simply a blank. Everything that mattered. Except Johnny. Only with him did she feel anchored in reality.

Ann and Jodie shared concerned glances and a silent communication. They probably knew Marla's story; the whole town probably did by now.

"Look, honey, if you need a couple of free spirits as stand-in sisters to lean on while you're trying to sort yourself out, we'd be happy to volunteer."

"She's free-spirited," Ann insisted. "I'm absolutely levelheaded."

"And boring," Jodie countered.

"I'm also smarter than you are."

"How can that be? We're identical."

"I was born first."

"You don't know that."

The two of them sparred back and forth good-naturedly as though they'd been doing it all their lives and had built a solid foundation of love. Marla couldn't imagine any two people she'd more enjoy having as sisters. But they belonged to each other; she was an outsider.

Right about then, two families arrived at the shack to order a half-dozen hot dogs each plus soft drinks. They were soon followed by a steady stream of lunchtime customers, keeping Marla too busy to do much thinking about her fears.

WHEN THE SOFTBALL GAME finished—the teens the victors as Johnny had predicted—Johnny came to claim Marla for lunch. A new shift of volunteers took over the duties at the snack shack to help raise money for youth programs.

"Are you sure you should've been on your feet so long?" he asked.

"It was only for an hour or so. I liked helping out." And liked working with Ann and her sister, she thought. Although she had to admit her back had begun to ache in the past few minutes. She'd be glad to sit a while. She had a feeling her baby would be arriving sooner rather than later. The doctor had said it could be any time now.

"Mama's got everything set up in the shade over there." Taking her hand, he led her across the grass toward two towering oak trees and a picnic table loaded with food.

"I wish you'd let me bring something to contribute to the picnic. I'm embarrassed—"

"Don't be. There's nothing Mama likes more than feeding her whole clan."

From the look of the heaping pans of spicy fried

chicken, cheese enchiladas, black beans, tortillas and a giant fruit salad, Dolores was prepared to feed an entire army. Johnny filled a plate to overflowing for Marla and then helped her to sit down on a blanket beneath one of the oak trees.

"You're going to need a crane to get me up again," she warned, settling herself against the tree.

"The city yard has a backhoe they use to scoop up rock slides that block the roads. Will that do?"

She smacked him playfully on the arm. "You didn't have to agree with me."

His low rumble of laughter was like warm molasses rolling sweetly over her.

While the children got their food, they relinquished Beau to Marla's care. Worn out by the excitement, the puppy collapsed on the blanket beside her. Idly, she patted his head. His tail scarcely twitched.

"This is wonderful," she said, enjoying the fresh air and the sight of dozens of families playing together. "Did your family go on a lot of picnics when you were a child?" Johnny's background was as much of a blank to Marla as her own was. She wanted to know the details, the experiences that had molded him into such a fine, strong man.

Frowning, he concentrated on eating his chicken leg before he responded. "I guess you could say we picnicked practically every day until I was about thirteen."

"Every day?"

"My father was a migrant farmworker. We'd start out in Oxnard in the spring working the strawberry fields, Mama and all us kids working beside him. Then we'd move north with the crops, picking fruit, and in late summer we'd work our way south again, harvesting grapes and breaking our backs on late-season tomatoes. We ate most of our meals off the back of a truck in the blazing sun—assuming my father had found work. Which didn't always happen.''

Marla was stunned by the revelation. ''The girls picked crops, too?''

''Except for Loretta. She's the youngest and was about six when we finally moved here, too young to be much use in the fields. Dad had finally gotten a steady job scrubbing toilets and washing dishes at Frederico's Cantina. That lasted about two years before he had a heart attack.''

Reaching out, she took his hand and brought it to her face, rubbing her cheek along the back. ''Oh, Johnny, I'm so sorry. How on earth did your mother manage after that?''

''She talked her way into taking over his job. And when that wasn't enough to keep us fed and a roof over our heads, she got a second job doing housekeeping at a couple of the motels down by the beach, cleaning up after the tourists.''

''She must be an amazing woman.''

''She is.'' Closing his hand around hers, he toyed with the diamond ring on her finger. ''Not exactly the life of Riley.'' He said it as though he were ashamed his family had been poor. Surely that was why he'd seemed so evasive when she asked if he'd ever owned pets as a child. His family couldn't afford to.

"Having money doesn't guarantee happiness." The flashes of insight she'd had led her to believe her childhood hadn't been all that happy, though she didn't sense she'd wanted for anything material. "I do know your father would be proud of what you've done with your life, and your mother loves you and your sisters to distraction. I'd say they've given you a fine legacy." The kind she'd like to pass on to her daughter.

"You're right." He returned the favor by kissing the back of her hand, sending a shimmer of warmth through her. "Say, by going off to the snack shop, you missed seeing my grand-slam home run."

"I did?"

"Yeah." He grinned at her, his mood shifting. "I was looking around the bleachers for you and I struck out without even seeing the ball. Otherwise it would have been a homer."

"Oh, you," she laughed. "And here I thought with all those trophies on the mantel, you were a big-time jock."

"I am when you're not distracting me."

"I'll keep that in mind." But her heart warmed with the knowledge that he'd been thinking of her when he should have been concentrating on the game. If she belonged nowhere else in the world, she wanted to belong to Johnny Fuentes, her husband.

AFTER LUNCH, DRIVEN BY the nearly perpetual need to visit the rest room, Marla made her way across the park to the gray-block building that sat hunched under a massive oak tree.

"I've gotta say you're the best-kept secret in town."

Marla turned toward the woman's voice, her eyes adjusting slowly to the dim light inside the rest room. Since there was no one else in the building, she assumed the redheaded stranger had to be speaking to her, though why her tone was so sarcastic Marla couldn't imagine.

"I beg your pardon?"

"Johnny let everybody think he was single, for God's sake, and then up you pop out of the blue. And pregnant to boot."

Recognition shot through Marla. This was the woman Johnny had been talking to earlier. "I don't know what you're talking about."

"Where'd he have you stashed, honey? Down in L.A. where he was playing cops and robbers?" She cocked one hip and fluffed her short hair with her hand. "You finally make him own up to being a daddy?"

With all the dignity she could muster, Marla swept past the woman and entered a stall, carefully locking the door. She stood rigidly at attention, praying the woman would go away, would stop talking. Would stop saying such awful things. Her stomach knotted.

"And snooty, too, huh? Guess he thought a waitress wasn't good enough for the big-time chief of po-lice."

Marla was going to be sick but with something

much worse than morning sickness. She was going to be sick at heart. Had Johnny been ashamed of her? Was that why no one in town knew her?

Except the mailman, she thought wildly, trying to reassure herself that she existed as Johnny's wife. *Mr. and Mrs. John Fuentes.*

"Well, you can tell him for me, Tina Tucker has never in her life stooped low enough to mess with a married man. And I sure as hell ain't gonna be his little tootsie on the side, either." There was a pause, then sandaled footsteps slapped out of the building.

To prevent a sob, Marla covered her mouth with her hand. What was the woman talking about? Had she and Johnny been lovers? Had he deceived and betrayed Marla in the same way that...? The image of that tall, brown-haired man leaped into her head again, making her temple throb.

She shoved the thought aside. Johnny couldn't be like that.

As she left the rest room, she walked straight ahead toward the spot where the Fuentes family was gathered, looking neither left nor right. She didn't want to see that woman again. Not today. Not ever. But she needed some answers.

Sitting down beside Johnny on a picnic bench, she said as casually as she could, "I saw a friend of yours in the ladies' room."

"Yeah? Who?"

"Tina Tucker."

He didn't blink an eye, showed no hint of embarrassment. "She's a waitress at the coffee shop in town. Nice lady."

Marla didn't think so. She thought Tina Tucker was jealous and vindictive. "Did you used to date her?"

"We went out a couple of times."

So that much was true. "Did you sleep with her?"

Slowly, he raised his dark eyebrows. "What did she say to you, kitten?"

"She said you'd been keeping me stashed somewhere. That you'd been keeping me a secret."

Gently, he brushed a few strands of wayward hair back from her face. "Look around. My family's here and half the town. Does it look like I'm keeping you a secret?"

No, it didn't. But that didn't explain why she seemed such a stranger to all these people whom she ought to know well. She was about to ask a few more probing questions when Beau managed to escape Michele's youthful supervision and bounded across the grass, leaping into Marla's lap and licking her face.

In spite of her troubling thoughts, she had to laugh at his clownish antics. By the time she calmed Beau and young Nick had claimed him for another walk around the park, Johnny was talking with the man who'd been introduced before the game as the mayor of Mar del Oro. Her questions would have to wait for another time.

JOHNNY WAS GETTING himself in deeper by the minute. He could feel it coming—the disappointment, the sense of loss when the time came that he had to let Marla go.

At the picnic, she'd seemed too much a part of his family, too comfortable with his friends in del Oro. That wasn't going to last when she figured out that she came from a far classier background than a migrant farmworker's family. She'd never be satisfied with the modest life-style he could offer.

Not that it mattered. Marla belonged to another man, a wealthy man who had given her a diamond worth half of Johnny's annual salary.

Later that night as he leaned back in the recliner, he flicked the remote control through the TV channels looking for something worth watching. Beau was contentedly chewing on Johnny's favorite pair of slippers, or at least what used to be his favorite. And Marla was at the kitchen table working on a new set of miniatures, this time figures from the Revolutionary War—British redcoats.

"Oh, my," she cried suddenly.

He glanced over his shoulder, figuring she'd probably given one of the soldiers the wrong color uniform. "What's wrong?"

"I think my water broke."

"Huh?" He leaped to his feet. "Are you sure?"

Her eyes were wide, her cheeks flushed. "It's that or my bladder's sprung a major leak." She tried for a smile.

He wasn't going to panic. Women had babies all the time. They'd been doing it for thousands of years.

"Should we head out to the hospital?" he asked calmly.

"No, let's just see what—" She bent over nearly double, groaning. "Oh, my God…"

Now he was going to panic. "I'll get your suitcase. You meet me at the car. And breathe. Remember to breathe."

Caught up in the excitement, Beau abandoned Johnny's slipper and bounded around the room barking, tail wagging, ready to play.

Racing down the hall to the bedroom, Johnny snatched up the small suitcase she'd packed days ago and headed for the front door. He was trained to handle emergencies. He could do this. It wasn't like he was really Marla's husband or about to be a new daddy. He was under control.

He hopped into his police car, turned the ignition and switched on the flashing emergency lights. As he pulled out of the driveway, he glanced toward the passenger side of the car and slammed on the brakes.

Dammit all!

He'd forgotten Marla!

NO RISK, NO OBLIGATION TO BUY...NOW OR EVER!

GUARANTEED

PLAY "ROLL A DOUBLE" AND YOU GET FREE GIFTS! HERE'S HOW TO PLAY:

1. Peel off label from front cover. Place it in space provided at right. With a coin, carefully scratch off the silver dice. Then check the claim chart to see what we have for you – TWO FREE BOOKS and a mystery gift – ALL YOURS! ALL FREE!

2. Send back this card and you'll receive brand-new Harlequin American Romance® novels. These books have a cover price of $3.99 each in the U.S. and $4.50 each in Canada, but they are yours to keep absolutely free.

3. There's no catch. You're under no obligation to buy anything. We charge nothing – ZERO – for your first shipment. And you don't have to make any minimum number of purchases – not even one!

4. The fact is, thousands of readers enjoy receiving books by mail from the Harlequin Reader Service®. They like the convenience of home delivery...they like getting the best new novels BEFORE they're available in stores...and they love our discount prices!

5. We hope that after receiving your free books you'll want to remain a subscriber. But the choice is yours – to continue or cancel any time at all! So why not take us up on our invitation, with no risk of any kind. You'll be glad you did!

THIS MYSTERY BONUS GIFT
WILL BE YOURS __FREE__ WHEN
YOU PLAY "ROLL A DOUBLE"

"ROLL A DOUBLE!"

Place label here

SCRATCH HERE

?

SEE CLAIM CHART BELOW

354 HDL CQV3

154 HDL CQVH
(H-AR-08/99)

YES! I have placed my label from the front cover into the space provided above and scratched off the silver dice to reveal a double. Please send me all the gifts for which I qualify. I understand that I am under no obligation to purchase any books, as explained on the back and on the opposite page.

Name:
(PLEASE PRINT)

Address: _____ Apt.#: _____

City: _____ State/Prov.: _____ Postal Zip/Code: _____

CLAIM CHART

🎲🎲	**2 FREE BOOKS PLUS MYSTERY BONUS GIFT**
🎲🎲	**2 FREE BOOKS**
🎲🎲	**1 FREE BOOK**

CLAIM NO.37-829

PRINTED IN U.S.A.

The Harlequin Reader Service® — Here's how it works:

Accepting your 2 free books and mystery gift places you under no obligation to buy anything. You may keep the books and gift and return the shipping statement marked "cancel." If you do not cancel, about a month later we'll send you 4 additional novels and bill you just $3.34 each in the U.S., or $3.71 each in Canada, plus 25¢ delivery per book and applicable taxes if any.* That's the complete price and — compared to the cover price of $3.99 in the U.S. and $4.50 in Canada — it's quite a bargain! You may cancel at any time, but if you choose to continue, every month we'll send you 4 more books, which you may either purchase at the discount price or return to us and cancel your subscription.

*Terms and prices subject to change without notice. Sales tax applicable in N.Y. Canadian residents will be charged applicable provincial taxes and GST.

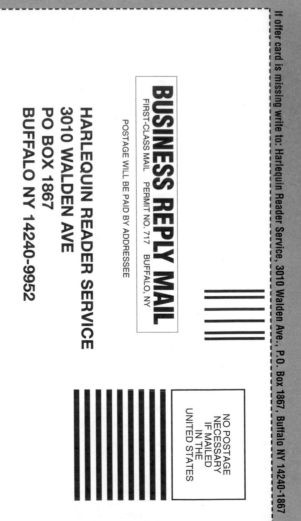

If offer card is missing write to: Harlequin Reader Service, 3010 Walden Ave., P.O. Box 1867, Buffalo NY 14240-1867

BUSINESS REPLY MAIL
FIRST-CLASS MAIL   PERMIT NO. 717   BUFFALO, NY

POSTAGE WILL BE PAID BY ADDRESSEE

HARLEQUIN READER SERVICE
3010 WALDEN AVE
PO BOX 1867
BUFFALO NY 14240-9952

NO POSTAGE
NECESSARY
IF MAILED
IN THE
UNITED STATES

Chapter Eight

"Come on, Daddy, let's get you in there to help Mama. We don't want her to have to do all the work."

The obstetric nurse propelled Johnny along the hospital corridor before he could object that he wasn't the baby's father. He wasn't sure she would care. Her job was to get someone in the labor room to coach Marla through the delivery. He'd been elected.

He found Marla propped up in a narrow bed.

"How's it going, kitten?" he asked, taking her hand. She'd changed from her street clothes into a pastel gown with tiny tulips on it, and she looked pale, a sheen of perspiration edging her forehead.

She squeezed his hand hard. "Not too bad so far. The pains are about three minutes apart now."

Good God! The contractions had gone from ten minutes apart when they left home to only three minutes in the time it had taken Johnny to fill out the necessary forms and officially get Marla registered and admitted to the hospital. The baby was determined to be born in a hurry.

"Where's the doctor?" he asked.

"I'm not dilated a whole lot yet. She'll be here later, they said."

Johnny scowled. "They can't just leave you alone like this."

She smiled. "I'm not alone. I have you with me. That's all I need."

Instinctively, he bent to press a kiss to her forehead. "You're going to be fine, kitten. So's the baby."

"I know." The muscles around her eyes tightened and her lips thinned as a contraction grabbed her. "Don't let go of me," she whispered, more groan than cry.

What was he supposed to do now? He'd noticed a Lamaze tape at home, one from the library, assumed she'd been watching it. He should have watched it with her. Should have prepared himself to be the one she relied on to help her through the birthing. But he'd been so damn sure her husband would be with her when this day arrived.

"Tell me what to do, kitten. Tell me and I'll do it." If she'd said to leap out the window, he would have done it, would have done anything to save her from the pain that was contorting her beautiful features.

"I need to focus on something. And breathe."

"Focus on me, kitten. I'm right here."

Her gaze bored into his, her eyes bright and as blue-green as the sea. When the pain eased, she smiled wanly. "Thank you for being here."

"This is where I belong." It was a lie and he knew

it. But it felt right that he was holding Marla's hand, helping her to give birth to her baby daughter. Not *his* baby daughter, but hers and another man's.

Regret slid through him.

"I think it's going to be a long night," she said.

No longer than the day when he'd have to give her up.

As each hour passed, the pains got harder, the intervals between them shorter. And Johnny sweated more profusely, as though he were doing the work himself. And he wished he were. Anything to ease the agony Marla was going through.

But she never did more than groan softly. She just kept staring at him, focusing on him and smiling weakly between contractions as if she were trying to give him a dose of the courage he lacked and she had in such abundance.

She breathed and squeezed his hand so hard he thought his bones were going to crack. He counted for her. He labored with her through every contraction, his own body aching with the strain. And he silently prayed as he hadn't since the night his father died.

He swore to God he'd never put a woman through this ordeal. He bargained with Him that he'd pay any price if only Marla didn't have to go through so much pain—even losing her to another man.

The doctor showed up, a sparse woman of about sixty, and peered under Marla's sheet-draped legs. Johnny kept his eyes averted.

"You're doing fine, Marla," Dr. Stevens announced. "We're almost there. Next time, I want you to push."

At some unseen signal, more nurses arrived in the room and an incubator was rolled inside. Was there something wrong? Were they expecting a problem? For Marla's sake, Johnny kept his questions to himself. He didn't want to worry her. Not now. Besides, he was doing enough worrying for the both of them.

"All right, let's get our daddy over here so he can catch his little bundle of joy," the doctor ordered.

"No, I can't—"

"Yes," Marla whispered, another contraction building. She started to breathe hard. "I want you to. I want you to be the first to hold our baby."

Our baby. God help him, how could he say no? She was counting on him to do the right thing, behave the way a loving husband would behave. And a loving father.

The doctor had him stand right beside her, facing Marla's bent legs. He didn't want to look, didn't want to note the intimacy of his position. He wasn't her husband, couldn't be her husband.

"See how the baby's crowning?" the doctor asked.

Johnny did. He swallowed hard.

Marla gave a sharp cry.

"Let's give a really big push. That's right. She's on her way now."

He heard Marla panting and crying all at once. He wanted to help her, wanted to stop the pain.

"One more time, Marla. You're doing fine." The doctor worked to ease the baby free. "As soon as this little darling is out, I'm going to hand her to you, Daddy. Use both hands just like you were going to catch a football. A soft touch, if you please.''

Marla screamed.

Like a slick football, the baby slid out, the doctor guiding the infant from Marla's womb right into his waiting hands.

''Meet your daddy, sweetheart,'' the doctor said, a smile in her voice. ''I'll give you exactly two seconds before you have him wrapped around your little finger.''

It didn't even take that long. The fierce protectiveness he'd felt for Marla was a thousand times more potent with this tiny creature in his hands. He wanted to give her the moon and stars; he wanted to run off every acne-faced teenager who showed up asking her for a date. He wanted a chance to love her mother.

Emotion filled his chest and burned in his throat. None of that was going to come true.

''All righty, let's have a look here and then we'll give Mama a chance.''

The doctor lifted the baby away, leaving Johnny's hands and heart empty. A few short minutes later, she placed the baby in Marla's arms while Johnny stood beside her.

There were tears in her eyes that matched his own. Though her hair was limp with sweat and there were bruises of fatigue under her eyes, Johnny didn't think he'd ever seen a woman who was more beautiful. Or more courageous.

"Isn't she beautiful?" Marla said, gazing at her child.

"You're the one who's beautiful," he said.

She smiled at him sweetly before returning to her examination of her baby. "I think she has your eyes."

He knew that wasn't true and needed to make light of her comment. He couldn't have her believing a lie—*another* lie. "What? Squinty?"

She laughed and pursed her lips as though the laughter hurt. "Well, at least you can't argue that she has your hair."

The dark cap of hair was stuck wetly to the baby's head, "Thanks, I think. I was kind of hoping she'd be blond like you."

"Looks like your mama is going to get her way," Marla said. "She definitely looks like a Teresa Caitlin Fuentes, don't you think? Terri, for short."

The lump in his throat was so huge it nearly closed off his breathing. "Perfect."

FATIGUE AND EUPHORIA mixed in a pleasant cocktail as Marla woke up several hours later. Johnny had gone home to get some sleep and feed the dog. In the crib next to her bed, Terri slept tightly bundled in a blanket, a tiny pink stocking cap on her head.

Fascinated by the way the baby made sucking motions with her mouth even in sleep and the dime-size pug nose she periodically wrinkled, Marla was reluctant to close her eyes long enough to get the rest she needed. What a priceless gift Terri was. Perfect in every way. Just like Johnny, her blue knight.

Tears stung at the backs of her eyes while apprehension tightened in her chest. If she'd been unlovable in the past, a snob or worse, did she deserve to be loved now? Could this soul-deep joy possibly last?

The image of a man came to her, tall and slender with saddle-brown hair and a counterfeit smile. He was laughing at her, mocking her. Tears of humiliation slid down Marla's cheeks. She didn't want to know that man, didn't want him to hurt her.

There was a knock on the open door and Dolores walked into the room. "What is this? Johnny's girl is crying?"

"Oh, Mama..." Marla sobbed.

As though Marla were one of her own children, Dolores sat down on the edge of the bed and took Marla in her arms. Her heavy breasts cushioned Marla, her strong arms embraced her. "It's all right, *mi hija,* my child. All women cry after they have a baby, *sí?* They're happy and sad and frightened all at once."

Marla was frightened, lost. But here in Mar del Oro, in Mama Fuentes's arms and Johnny's life, she felt that she'd been found. Dear heaven, she didn't want to lose that.

Dolores patted her back and smoothed her hair. "The baby is good, *sí?*"

"She's perfect." Pulling herself together, Marla found a tissue on the nightstand and wiped her eyes. "That was so silly of me. I didn't mean to turn into a water fountain."

"Bah. It is nothing. We all do that. It's part of

being a woman.'' She patted Marla's cheek with her callused hand. ''Now, let me see my new grandchild.''

''We named her Terri—Teresa Caitlin. I hope you approve.''

Nodding, Mama's chin quivered ever so slightly. ''I had a great-aunt who lived in a very small village in the mountains. Every day she would walk five miles to fill her jug with water and then walk home again. She was a very strong woman.'' She leaned over the crib and lovingly caressed Terri's cheek with the back of her fingers. ''Baby Teresa will be strong like her.''

''She'll grow up proud of her ancestry. I promise.''

''And I will be proud of her.''

BY EVENING, MARLA'S ROOM had the look of a florist shop. In addition to the flowers Rita had brought during the afternoon, Dora had sent an azalea plant and Marla's ''stand-in'' sisters, Ann and Jodie, had sent an arrangement of bright summer blooms. She'd never imagined the pleasure of having so many friends and family members; perhaps she hadn't known it was possible.

Then Johnny showed up with an armful of gladioli in every color of the rainbow and a teddy bear the size of a five-year-old child. She nearly burst into tears again as she had that morning with his mother. Her wretched hormones must be acting up.

''They're lovely,'' she said as he shifted the other

flowers on the bed table around to make room for his vase.

"Looks like my idea of bringing flowers wasn't particularly original."

"Everything you do is special, Johnny. Terri's going to love the teddy bear and will probably think it's her big brother." He was such a dear man, her heart was overflowing with love. "I don't know how I was so lucky that I found you."

He cocked an eyebrow at her and smiled. "That's what happens when a pretty woman goes walking on the beach alone. Some guy's likely to come along and pick her up." He bent to give her a fleeting kiss. "Doctor says you and Terri can come home in the morning."

"I'll be ready. I'm really tired of being poked and prodded. Hospitals are not my favorite places."

The baby stirred, making tiny mewling sounds, and opened her eyes. They were big and round and a deep blue. Her gaze darted from one place to the next until it finally landed on Johnny, or seemed to. Then she let out a howl.

"Hey, kid, don't yell at me," Johnny said, unable to keep himself from laughing. "I didn't make the world such a tough place to live in."

"I don't think that's a political commentary she's making. It's more like she's hungry." Marla pressed the button to raise her bed to a more upright position. "Would you get her for me, please?"

"Uh, sure." Except for last night when he'd caught Terri at the moment of her birth, it had been a long time since he'd held a baby. Then it had been his sister's, not one who was supposed to be his own. And not younger than twenty-four hours old.

While he hesitated, Terri continued to plead her case for ending world hunger.

"Johnny?"

"I'm not sure how to grab hold of her," he confessed.

"She won't break, silly."

Johnny wasn't so sure. But he did know enough not to let her head flop back, so he picked her up gingerly using both hands. She barely weighed more than a football, although he'd been told she was over seven pounds.

"Tuck her in the crook of your arm so she can cuddle against your chest."

He did as instructed, and the baby turned her head, nuzzling her mouth against his shirt. A band of love tightened around his chest and he swallowed hard. "Gotta tell you, little muffin, you're gonna find a dry well there."

Laughing a sweet sound, Marla lifted her arms for the baby. "I'm probably better equipped in this case for what she's after than you are."

Almost enviously, he placed Terri in Marla's arms. He watched in fascination as she pulled back her gown and held the baby to her breast—as white as ivory and delicately laced with blue veins. His body reacted with a swift surge of desire at the intimacy of the scene.

"I'd better close the door," he said, his voice a hoarse whisper.

"No one can see past the curtain. Stay. Sit here beside us." She patted the bed.

He should look away. In spite of her request, he ought to leave the room. He had no right to be there. But the erotic sight of Marla's naked breast drew him like a con artist to a sting. He couldn't resist. He wasn't noble enough to turn away. All he could think about was how the weight of her breasts, heavy with milk, would feel in his palms.

Now that he knew she wasn't the suspect in the series of armed robberies in Los Angeles, he should be pursuing other means of discovering her identity. Spreading her picture on the TV news. Checking her fingerprints with licensing departments in other states.

He didn't want to do any of that.

He wanted to take her and the baby home with him, make them his family. He wanted to watch Terri grow into a young woman. He wanted to love Marla. Forgetting his vow never to put a woman through the agony of childbirth, he wanted to make more babies with her. And he didn't have the right.

Despite that, he sat down beside her.

"Now bend closer."

He arched his brows. "Closer?"

"I think you deserve a kiss for being such a good daddy. And I deserve a little reward, too."

Oh, man, how could he tell her no?

The taste of her lips was as honeyed as mother's milk and he hungered for their sweetness. They molded to his as he felt the soft thrust of her tongue. His body clenched. Aching need arose in him.

Her free hand looped behind his neck, her fingers teasing at his nape. How, he wondered, could a woman who'd just had a baby—and that baby was in her arms—arouse him so thoroughly? But Marla did. And now sure as hell wasn't the time to do anything about it.

He broke the kiss.

Taking a deep breath, she grinned at him impishly. "That was quite a reward, Mr. Fuentes."

"Yeah."

"They tell me after a woman has a baby, her hormonal activity is very high."

"Really?"

"I think I can already vouch for that. You definitely turned me on."

"Yeah, well, guess we'd better cool it, right?" He backed away and then stood. She'd shaken him with her kiss more than he'd care to admit.

"I'll be counting the days till we can make love again."

He swallowed hard. Before that happened, he'd have to tell her they weren't married—never had been.

"Oh, by the way—" she shifted her hold on the baby "—I filled out most of the information for the birth certificate, but I couldn't remember your middle name."

The birth certificate! She'd list him as the baby's father. Damn! Why hadn't he thought of that?

"Officially, I'm Juan Eduardo José Fuentes, named for my father." And he couldn't very well *officially* be Terri's father. Some other man had the claim to that title.

"That's nice." She smiled at him. "The form's on the table there somewhere. The nurse wanted it back as soon as possible. Could you take care of it?"

"Sure." He found it under a box of tissues. She'd printed his first and last name clearly, boldly, and he wished it were true. He'd feel so filled with pride to be Terri's father, he'd probably burst. But wishing wouldn't make it so.

He'd have to talk with Doc Bernie and get the form changed to "father unknown" for the time being. Marla could amend the form later. After she'd gotten together with her husband again.

That bit of reality stuck in Johnny's craw like a jagged chicken bone. How would he ever be able to say goodbye to either Marla or her baby?

AFTER ONLY TWO DAYS, he'd become pretty damn good at this diapering business.

"Haven't I, little muffin girl?" Bending over, he blew a soft kiss to her belly. In a delayed reaction, she squirmed and waved her arms. "If you're going to be a jock, we've got to work on your reaction time. You're never going to get off the blocks fast enough."

"I'm not sure she's ready for a hundred-yard dash quite yet." Dressed in her robe and slippers, Marla came up beside him and slipped her arm around his waist, leaning against his shoulder as she gazed down at her baby.

"Hey, I thought you were napping. I was going to try to keep her quiet while you got a few more winks. You had a long night." Rationalizing that a new mother shouldn't be left on her own, he'd taken a few days off to help her out. Despite their combined lack of sleep, he was enjoying playing a daddy. But deep in his gut, he knew it couldn't last. Somewhere out there, Terri had a real father. Johnny ought to be moving mountains to find him.

He wasn't.

"As soon as she cries, my milk comes in. Besides, you have to be exhausted, too."

"It's amazing what a tyrant such a cute little bundle can be."

As he finished diapering and pulling Terri's nightgown into place, Marla asked, "Do you think her color is right?"

"Looks fine to me." Cute as a muffin.

"You don't think she's a little yellow?"

He cocked his head and studied the baby. "Yellow's not good?" How the heck should he know? And how was he supposed to tell if her complexion was off a shade or two?

"Rita gave me a book on raising babies. I think Terri may have jaundice."

Fear sliced through Johnny's chest. "Is that bad?" He'd move heaven and earth to see she got the best medical attention available. If they didn't have the necessary specialists here in del Oro, he'd—

"Maybe I'd better call the doctor to make sure," Marla said.

"No, I'll take her into the office. The doctor can't diagnose over the phone. This could be an emergency."

"Johnny, I think you're overreacting. If Terri was really sick, she wouldn't be so lively."

"But maybe this jaundice stuff is what's keeping her awake half the night." He bundled the baby in a soft blanket and handed her over to Marla. "You go ahead and nurse her. I'll call the doctor's office and tell them I'll be there in half an hour, forty-five minutes max."

"I'll have to get dressed."

"No, I'll take her. You need your rest."

Marla looked doubtful. "Are you sure you can manage on your own?"

"Hey, how hard is it to put a baby in a car seat and haul her off to the doctor? Remember me? I'm your blue knight."

"Right." Marla smiled, but somehow Johnny didn't think it was a total vote of confidence.

DIAPER BAG. EXTRA BOTTLE of formula in case Terri got hungry. Pacifier. A spare set of clothes in case she barfed...or worse. Sweater. More diapers. A set of plastic keys for her to hang on to, not that she had a real good grip yet on anything except her mother's bosom. A car seat that weighed as much as a ten-year-old kid.

An hour later as he backed out of the driveway in

his police car, Terri buckled up in the back seat facing the rear, Johnny was confident he could do this. He could even glance over his shoulder to keep an eye on her. Men, he reasoned, had been dads almost as long as women had been moms. The job didn't require any biological connection to the kid. Just a willingness to take responsibility.

Still not looking terribly confident, Marla waved from the front porch as Johnny headed down the street. He probably should have driven his civilian car, but the front tires had worn smooth and one had a slow leak he hadn't gotten around to fixing yet. With Terri along, he felt much safer driving a vehicle that had had regular maintenance. These days, Terri's well-being was right at the top of the list. And as the chief of police, he was authorized to use a police vehicle for private business—one of the perks of the job.

But tomorrow he'd take his Toyota in for new tires and full servicing. No telling when he might need it in an emergency. He was, after all, a family man now—at least temporarily, he conceded.

He'd reached the freeway underpass when the police radio sputtered awake.

"To all units," Patty's voice announced from dispatch. "Two suspects from the 211 at Burger King are reported fleeing northbound on Highway 1 in a white minivan, license number beginning three-Roger-Roger. Suspects are described as white males, ages twenty to twenty-five. The younger suspect is wearing a green baseball cap."

On the freeway above him, Johnny spotted a white

van heading northbound well in excess of eighty miles an hour—probably the suspects.

He swore softly under his breath, switched on his siren and lights, then grabbed the mike as he wheeled the car up the on-ramp. He couldn't ignore fleeing suspects. "This is unit one. I have suspect vehicle in sight north of the Main Street on-ramp and am pursuing."

"Roger, copy that, unit one."

"I've got a civilian in the car, Dispatch. A very small one. I'll need backup. In a hurry, if you please."

"Understood, unit one. Unit two is en route."

He got close enough to the minivan to confirm the license number, called it in and then eased back, keeping the vehicle in sight. The suspects didn't have anywhere to go except to stay on the highway, and Johnny didn't want to risk a high-speed accident with Terri in the car.

He glanced over his shoulder at the baby in the back seat. If the situation hadn't been so serious, he would have laughed out loud. Terri's arms were waving like a symphony conductor's, and if he wasn't mistaken, she had a big, toothless grin. By damn! She loved the siren. Maybe she'd grow up to be a cop.

The suspect vehicle began to slow just as unit two appeared beside Johnny. He waved Officer Maloney on ahead and slowed even further. This was, after all, supposed to be a vacation day for Johnny. He'd let his troops handle the arrest. At the moment, he had more important things on his mind—like getting Terri to the doctor's office.

When he reached a break in the median strip, he made a U-turn and headed back toward town, allowing himself a smile of satisfaction. Not many three-day-old babies could brag that they'd been involved in a high-speed chase and helped catch a couple of suspected felons.

By the time he got to the doctor's office, Terri was sound asleep, exhausted by all the excitement. Dr. Stevens assured him in a mildly condescending way that all new parents tended to panic. Jaundice was nothing to worry about. He and Marla simply needed to place Terri in the sunshine for a few minutes a day—bare naked—and give her a few ounces of water periodically to be sure she was getting enough liquid.

Okay, he and Marla could handle that. Being a parent wasn't that hard.

By the time he changed Terri's diaper, packed up the diaper bag, found the missing pacifier when she started to fuss and got back to his car, Johnny decided being a dad—or mom—was a lot tougher than it looked.

When he arrived home, he was feeling a little sheepish about overreacting. And wasn't about to admit he'd been involved in a high-speed chase with Terri in the car.

"What did the doctor say?" Marla asked, her forehead creased with worry. "You were gone so long."

"Well, you know these things take time—making a diagnosis, I mean."

"Then it's something more than jaundice?"

"No, no. You were right." Squatting, he juggled Terri as he spread a receiving blanket on a square of sunshine near the sliding glass door. Outside, Beau scratched on the window in a futile plea to come inside. "The doctor was glad I brought her in, though, just in case. She says we're supposed to sun her a few minutes every day and give her water."

"Really?" She sounded a bit smug. "That's just what Rita's baby-care book said. Guess you could've saved yourself the trip."

"It was probably best I took her in, just to be sure everything was okay." Laying Terri on the blanket, he unsnapped her sleeper and tugged it off. Her skin was the smoothest thing he'd ever felt.

Marla's hand rested on his shoulder. "Thank you."

Embarrassed, he stood. "You're right, I could've saved—"

"No, you were being cautious by seeing the doctor. We're both so new at this parenting business." Standing on tiptoe, she kissed him lightly, then linked her fingers with his. "I think I've wanted a baby to love all my life. I want to do it right."

"You will. You're a natural."

She worried her lower lip between her teeth. "I'm not so sure. I have the feeling... I don't think I was loved very much as a child."

"Are you remembering something specific from the past, or is it just a feeling?" And did that memory include another man who had more right to hold Marla than Johnny did?

"A feeling, mostly. But it makes me afraid I'm not capable of giving the unconditional love a child needs." Resting her head on his shoulder, she looked down at the sleeping baby. "Loving her seems to come so easily to you. Why is that?"

"Because she's part of you, kitten. How could I not love her?" He wanted to tell her that he'd always love Terri, that he'd be the best damn daddy in the world. But he wasn't likely to have that chance and he didn't have the courage to tell Marla about all his lies. Not yet.

She still wasn't ready to face the reality that would drive him from her life. But in his gut, he knew he was a thief, stealing a little more time with Marla.

Whispering a thank-you, she kissed him, a long and lingering kiss, and Johnny realized how easy it was to succumb to temptation.

BUT TWO WEEKS LATER, Johnny decided he'd procrastinated as long as he could, and he went to see Dr. Bernie. He didn't want to stop being Terri's dad, or Marla's husband, but he was running out of excuses for hiding the truth from her. He couldn't keep lying to her about their relationship. His feelings had grown too deep for that, and her questions had grown too frequent. *Vague* didn't even begin to cover his answers.

"Truthfully, I had thought she would recover her memory before this," Dr. Bernie said. He polished his glasses, putting them on again with care. "From a medical viewpoint—given her general good health and that of the baby—I can see no justification to continue as you have been."

Johnny could, but it sure as hell wasn't a noble reason. "So what do I do? Just blurt it out that we're total strangers and I've been lying to her for the past six weeks?"

"I'd say at this point you're on much closer terms than that of strangers."

He had that damn right! "So? It doesn't change the fact that I've lied to her."

"Seems to me, Johnny..." He took off his glasses again and wiped them. "With women, you're probably as diplomatic as any man I know. I'm sure you can break the news to her gently."

Johnny wasn't all that confident and he sure as hell wasn't looking forward to telling Marla what he'd done. From the beginning, he'd known he was bound to get into deep trouble with her. He hadn't been wrong.

Dispirited, he headed back to his office. At least he could put off the inevitable until dinnertime. Maybe he could get Mama to baby-sit Terri and he'd take Marla out somewhere nice. Bad news always went down easier over a good dinner and a glass of wine—or so he hoped.

Patty practically tackled him the moment he arrived at the office.

"They've found a car," she said.

"Car? What car?"

"A Mercedes, nearly new, about fifty yards offshore from Creek Canyon. Some kids who were scuba diving spotted it. It looks like it could have been in the water for several weeks. I've dispatched a patrol car.''

For a moment, Johnny couldn't speak and he had to swallow hard before he could get any words out. ''Victims inside?''

''The kids said they couldn't see anybody, but the driver's door was open.'' She shrugged though her worried expression mirrored his own. ''Do you think it's your, uh, wife's car?''

Johnny wasn't going to jump to any conclusions just yet. Car thieves had been known to dump cars off the cliff. The kids who'd found the vehicle could be wrong about how long it had been in the water. For that matter, the whole thing could be a teenage hoax.

''I'll check it out,'' he said grimly. In his gut, however, he knew whatever they found in the ocean, his charade as Marla's husband was about to end.

Federal Building, San Francisco

VISITING THE FEDERAL prosecutor's office was a little like showing up for the Inquisition. Tommy Tompkins straightened his tie before he stepped inside. It could have as easily been a noose.

Taking off her glasses, the prosecutor looked up at him. ''Well?''

''Our suspect purchased a house in San Luis Obispo. For cash. Escrow was set to close, but she never showed up to sign the final papers.''

"A diversion?"

"Possibly. We've alerted the Realtor and the escrow company as well as her bank in Marin, where she's still has more money in her accounts than I'll ever see in this lifetime. If she surfaces, we'll hear about it. You want us to put a hold on her accounts?"

The prosecutor considered that option. "I don't want her to know we've got her number. If she uses an ATM anywhere in the world, I want to be able to track her down. Let's leave her money alone until we get a handle on where she is. If she's still in the States, she'll leave a trail."

Tommy agreed. Though the suspect might have other funds stashed away, the temptation to get at her accounts locally would be overwhelming.

He'd long since learned that innate greed was the thing that most often led to a criminal's capture.

Chapter Nine

Marla heard Johnny's car pull up out front and smiled. He was home early.

Easing Terri away from her breast, she lifted her sated daughter to her shoulder and gently patted her back. She rocked back and forth, waiting for the first heart-stopping glimpse of her husband—her blue knight.

How often each day did she think about him, picturing his crooked smile and simpatico eyes? And how many times during the night did she relish the comfort and security of his warm embrace? And how many kisses had she teased him with—kisses that had grown more heated as the days passed?

The answer must be in the thousands.

Only the niggling fear that the person she had once been didn't deserve such happiness tempered her unbridled joy.

She glanced toward the fireplace mantel and her talisman, the medieval knight. As long as he was there, everything would be all right.

The front door opened and Johnny stepped inside,

his jacket slung over his shoulder, his expression grim. Her heart lurched. Something was terribly wrong.

The image of another time, another place, leaped into her mind. Two policemen that day, their expressions solemn as they stood on the brick porch before the massive front door. Why? What terrible thing had taken place?

"Johnny?" Her head began to throb; her breathing turned shallow.

His dark brows pulling together, he sat on the edge of the coffee table in front of her. He studied her with a curiously intense look as if he was about to interrogate her. But there was gentleness in his expression and concern, his dark eyes—as always—so simpatico.

Whatever he was about to say, she wanted to silence him, to stop the words she sensed would change her life forever.

"Some scuba divers found a car in the water about fifty yards offshore this morning, ten miles north of here. A Mercedes."

She stared at him, trying not to think—unable to think as she rocked slightly, soothing the sleeping baby in her arms. *A silver-gray Mercedes S500. Leather interior.* How would she know that? Why would she think that?

Forcefully, she blocked the image from her mind.

"The car looked like it'd been in the water for several weeks. It probably went into the drink about the time I found you walking on the beach."

How could Johnny have afforded a new Mercedes

for her? His civilian car, as he called it, was an aging Toyota that was most often left in the garage. Just two weeks ago, he'd purchased new tires, complaining about the price. A luxury car would be beyond—

"Does the name Victoria Stapleton mean anything to you?"

Denying the possibility, she shook her head. It wasn't her car. She was Marla Fuentes, Johnny's wife, Terri's mommy. She didn't want to be anyone else. She was happy here.

"How 'bout David Stapleton?"

Tall. Saddle-brown hair. "No," she whispered, pain piercing her temple like a medieval lance.

"The car was registered to David and Victoria Stapleton of Marin County, north of San Francisco. Have you ever been there?"

A Tudor-style house several times the size of Johnny's home—her *home.* "I don't remember."

"Kitten, I think you were driving that Mercedes the night of your accident. The left rear fender was hit by another vehicle. You probably spun out. I think you went off the road through a gap in the guardrail near Creek Canyon. It was high tide that night, and the currents probably pulled the car farther out into the ocean after you swam free, which is why we never spotted it." He rested his big, gentle hand on her knee, warm and reassuring. "I think you're Victoria Stapleton."

Helplessly, she shook her head again. "I'm your wife."

"No, kitten, you're not. You and I have never been married."

"How can you say such an awful thing?" She shot to her feet. She couldn't listen, didn't want to listen. "I thought we could grill some chicken breasts tonight. I made a really nice teriyaki sauce—"

Standing, he caught her arm, his strong hand with neatly trimmed fingernails closing around her. "Marla—kitten—we need to get to the bottom of this. You need to get your memory back."

Pulling her around, he hugged her and the baby in a bearlike embrace. His blue shirt felt smooth against her cheek and smelled faintly of the lemon detergent she'd used. Though he said he'd take his shirts to the laundry, she'd wanted to wash them herself. Iron them. Be a good wife to him.

A sob caught in her throat. "How can you say we aren't married?"

"Because it's true."

"The mailman knew I was Mrs. Fuentes. He saw my name on a letter." But there'd only been one, she realized desperately. No notes from friends. Not even a credit card bill.

"Seeing you here, he made the assumption that you're my wife."

Such a devastatingly simple answer. So obviously true. In that instant, the joy she'd clung to so tenaciously shattered like a fragile glass figurine crashing onto a tile floor. *She didn't deserve happiness.*

Confusion and anger mixed with despair and a terrible dark sense of betrayal. "Are you saying you've been lying to me all this time?"

"Dr. Bernie thought it was the best thing for you and the baby."

"That certainly gives new meaning to the term malpractice, doesn't it?" The bitter taste of deceit rose in her throat. The familiar flavor burned her tongue. She'd been betrayed before. But by whom?

"You were confused after the accident. You thought I was your husband. The doc was afraid if we told you the truth, you'd go into premature labor. Given your fragile condition, he didn't want to risk that."

She gaped at him, myriad emotions flitting through her head, her insides twisting in confusion. "Terri's almost three weeks old. It didn't occur to you to tell me the truth in all that time?"

"Yeah, it did."

"But you let me go on believing—"

"I'm sorry."

"We've been sleeping together, for God's sake. Every night you—"

"I know. I should have told you."

The baby managed a loud, very emphatic burp. Marla—how could she think of herself as Victoria when she couldn't recall being that person?—patted Terri's back and wiped the spittle from her chin with the corner of her receiving blanket.

She stopped, realization seeping into her ever more deeply, ever more painfully. "If you're not my husband... You're not Terri's father, are you?"

"No."

Oh, God, oh, God. How could he say that so easily? He'd walked Terri in the wee hours of the morning when she'd been fussy and Marla too tired to care for her. He'd raced her to the doctor's office over the least little fear or concern. He'd diapered her and rocked her. He'd been everything a father could be—except a real one.

Suddenly, she felt faint. "I put your name on her birth certificate." Johnny was the father she wanted for her baby, the only father she needed.

"Dr. Bernie fixed it. Temporarily. Until we find out for sure who her father is."

"Who?" She cleared the clog of emotion from her throat. "Who's her father?" Whom had Marla slept with, kissed, been held by? A man she couldn't remember.

No, she didn't *want* to remember. *The stranger with the saddle-brown hair.*

"I'm assuming, if that Mercedes is your car, that Terri's father is David Stapleton."

She fought a wave of nausea. "Was...was he in the car?"

"I don't know for certain. There was no sign of another victim."

"I was alone?"

He shrugged. "As near as we can tell."

"Are you sure I'm this...Victoria person?"

"The facts, the time line, all fit. But we didn't find any purse in the car with your ID or anything definitive like that. Though a purse could've easily been washed out of the car. There were suitcases in the trunk. I'm having my people go through them now.''

She shuddered at the invasion of her privacy— someone's privacy. ''If I have a husband…'' She had Johnny, the only husband she wanted, or at least she'd thought he was hers. ''Where is he?''

''That I don't know. No one filed a missing person report on you. Under normal circumstances, I'd expect a husband to begin worrying that you hadn't arrived at your destination, wherever that was.''

She searched her mind for some sense that this unknown husband of hers would care if she didn't make it home. All she felt was emptiness.

''And if he hoped I'd never come back? Maybe he was responsible for my going over the cliff.''

''I've been assuming it was a hit-and-run, a glancing blow the other driver may not have been aware of. It was a pretty foggy night.'' Johnny's forehead tugged into a thoughtful frown. ''If it was more than that—intentional—it'd be hard to prove after all these weeks. I also suppose it's possible you're divorced and not on close terms with your ex any longer. He might not know you're missing. But if that were true, the divorce would've been recent, considering the car was still registered in both your names.''

Johnny had been lying to her for weeks, no matter that he'd been doing it on doctor's orders. Could she believe him now when he told her he wasn't her husband? Yet it answered so many of the questions she'd been asking herself.

Why no one in town had known her.

Why her everyday clothes were missing from the closet.

And why the maternity clothes she did have weren't quite her style.

Awareness dawned. "I've been wearing Rita's hand-me-downs, haven't I?"

He nodded.

"Your family knew all along that we weren't married?" That news rocked her off her mental equilibrium once again. "Even your mother?" Dolores had been so kind, so accepting of "Marla" as her daughter-in-law. How could she have done that? Deceived her like all the others.

"By now, pretty much everyone in town has figured out what's been going on."

A flush that was both anger and embarrassment stole up her neck. "That we've been playing house. What a laugh they must gotten at my expense." Except for his girlfriend Tina, who hadn't been laughing at all.

"It hasn't been like that. Everyone's been concerned about you. They care, Marla. So do I."

The baby started to fuss, and Marla shifted Terri to her other shoulder. She closed her eyes. *Not Terri Fuentes. Caitlin Stapleton instead.* Dear heaven, it didn't seem possible. She'd been so proud, so happy to write Johnny's name on her baby's birth certificate. Now it was a lie.

"Here, let me take her," Johnny said.

"She's not yours."

"That doesn't mean I can't hold her. Or change the

fact that I've loved Terri from the moment she was born. Maybe even before that.''

But he didn't love Marla. Or Victoria. He wasn't her husband.

She let Johnny take Terri into his arms and felt the loss of the baby's warmth as though the sun had slipped behind a dark cloud. She leaned back against the kitchen counter for fear she'd collapse if she didn't have something to hang on to.

"What do I do now, Johnny? I still can't remember ever being anyone else." Only Johnny's wife. "Where do I go now?"

"I could call the local authorities in Marin to check out David Stapleton and ask some questions around town. But Dr. Bernie thinks it would be better if you went there and saw things for yourself. The house, the neighborhood. Your husband." Johnny glanced away, a muscle in his jaw ticking. "Doc figures there's a good chance your memory would return."

"What if I don't *want* to remember? What if my life was so awful that I'm better off forgetting.''

"You have to face the past, whatever it is. That's the only way you'll be able to go forward, kitten.''

Her chin trembled. The tears that had been threatening pooled in her eyes and spilled down her cheeks. Her happiness had been too good to last.

"Am I supposed to hop on a bus and show up at this man's house—a stranger's house—and announce I'm his long-lost wife, whom he didn't even bother to look for?''

"No, you're not going on your own. I'm going

with you. Whenever you think you're up to the trip. I'll arrange to take some time off.''

Marla turned away from him. She'd never be ready for a trip back into her past.

THAT NIGHT, JOHNNY SLEPT in the guest room, and without his warmth the ocean dampness crept under the covers to chill Marla. She had no recollection of ever sleeping with another man, of someone else holding her. But it must have happened. Terri was evidence of that.

If she had felt an emptiness before, now—without Johnny beside her—there was a dark void that stretched beyond the limits of the sea and sky. She had no one except her baby. She'd lost her anchor, felt more adrift than ever.

In spite of her stubborn refusal to cry, tears crept from beneath her eyelids to dampen her pillow. Torment filled the hollow of her chest. Somehow she had to find the courage to face David Stapleton, discover if he was the man with the saddle-brown hair and she was Victoria. Whatever the outcome of that meeting, she would have to go on with her life for Terri's sake.

Maybe the person she'd been didn't deserve happiness, but she did now. And so did her baby. She could only hope and pray that Johnny would be a part of her new life.

She wished to God the scuba divers had never found that car, wished things could have remained as they were. Wished she'd never heard the name of Victoria Stapleton.

Coward that she was, Marla put off the inevitable as long as she could, saying Terri was too young to travel. Johnny waited for her to make the decision.

Finally, on Terri's one-month birthday, he told her it was time to go.

RATHER THAN TAKING Highway 1, which was a slow drive under any circumstances, they cut over to San Luis Obispo to U.S. 101, the inland route. Until they reached the Bay area, the weather was hot, the Toyota's air conditioner barely keeping up with the heat of the sun blasting in the car windows.

Terri seemed to sense Marla's anxiety and began to fuss. In an effort to keep the baby occupied, Johnny stopped the car long enough for Marla to get into the back seat with her.

"What if we find out I'm an awful person?" she said, finally voicing one of her biggest fears.

Johnny's eyes met hers in the rearview mirror and the corners of his eyes crinkled with an encouraging smile. "Not possible, kitten."

"You can't be sure of that."

"I'm sure."

Despite her dread of what was to come and her knowledge that Johnny wasn't her husband, she marveled at how his words reassured her and his physical presence fascinated her. His broad shoulders tapered into a muscular neck; his dark hair was neatly trimmed but not so short as to be priggish. She was sick with the thought she might never again be allowed to run her fingers through the thick strands at his nape, disrupting their orderliness as he kissed her.

His hands on the steering wheel were both sure and strong as he turned off the highway north of San Francisco onto a winding road through wooded, upscale residential areas and a small village crowded with cars. She wished she could feel his hands on her, loving her, caressing her with the same gentle confidence he demonstrated when he held Terri. Now, if it turned out she was Victoria Stapleton, she might never have a chance.

She gritted her teeth against a new wave of sorrow.

The scenery looked vaguely familiar, though she could have traveled this way on a vacation or a weekend outing. It didn't necessarily mean she had lived here.

Or that she had a husband here.

A block off the main road, he pulled into a circular driveway in front of a Tudor-style house with a brick front porch. The yard was immaculately landscaped with flower beds in full summer bloom and a neat row of cypress trees providing a privacy screen from the neighbors.

Flashes of memory, like white-hot pokers, stabbed at her mind. The late-afternoon shadows blurred her perceptions, confusing her.

"I can't do this, Johnny. I can't just walk in there—"

"I'll be right beside you. I promise." Switching off the ignition, Johnny knew that was the only promise he could make. He'd stay with Marla—Victoria—

until she found her own place again. Her husband. And then he'd have to go.

He helped her and the baby out of the car and they walked up to the porch. The place looked like one of those damn English manor houses he'd seen on PBS, probably ten thousand square feet plus a four-car garage. He half expected the lord of the manor to show up at the door to claim his wife and throw Johnny, a peasant, off the estate. But he wouldn't go until he knew she was safe and learned why the hell her husband hadn't come looking for her.

He rang the doorbell. When no one answered, he took Marla's elbow and ushered her off the porch and around toward the side of the house. Hell, he was as nervous as a football quarterback who was down by ten points with less than two minutes to play. He'd been worrying about this trip for days. He didn't intend to leave without discovering if Marla was Victoria Stapleton, a woman who had a husband.

"What are you doing, Johnny?"

"We'll take a look around, that's all. Maybe you'll see something that looks familiar." In which case he'd lose her to some wealthy dude who obviously didn't give a damn about her.

"Or maybe we'll get shot for trespassing?"

He flashed her a grin. "I'm a cop. They wouldn't dare."

"You're not wearing your uniform, so how are they supposed to know that?" Holding Terri more tightly to her shoulder, Marla glared at him. "I'd just as soon my daughter didn't end up in jail for her one-month birthday party.''

''Not to worry. She's definitely a juvenile. Besides, I've got my ID and we're just going to take a peek inside. It's no big deal.'' At least he didn't think it would be, assuming one of the neighbors didn't spot them and call the cops. He didn't exactly have juris-diction in Marin County to do any investigating.

He found a set of French doors off the patio in back that didn't have curtains covering them.

''Take a look,'' he ordered.

Not entirely thrilled with his request, she peered in the window. He heard her make a choking sound and his heart sank. She'd seen something—something that she recognized.

The small sounds she was making became louder. She turned and tears were rolling down her cheeks. Oh, God! She'd remembered. He felt it in his gut, and something in his chest split apart. A broken heart, he realized.

''Johnny, take a look yourself.''

''I don't need to. If you recognize—''

''Look!'' It wasn't a polite command. In fact, it sounded more like a choked-off laugh. ''You won't believe what's in there.''

He frowned. What the hell was she talking about? Edging up to the window, he peered inside as Marla's laughter turned to uncontrollable giggles.

''Trust me, Johnny. This place seemed familiar to me at first, but I've never lived here. I couldn't. If that's how Victoria Stapleton decorates, I'm definitely not her. For which I am humbly grateful.''

Squinting, he looked around what he supposed was a family or game room. The tile floor was checkered in black, white and red like an oversize chess board; overhead, felt streamers in orange and vermilion draped down from an upstairs balcony. Instead of classy like Marla, it was…ghastly. Garish.

There was no possible way Marla had decorated that house, much less lived there. The relief he felt was like a cleansing tide, filling him with hope. She wasn't Victoria Stapleton.

''The car we found must not have been yours,'' he said.

Her lips twitched with the threat of a smile. ''Thank goodness.''

Which gave him a second mystery to solve. Why had a nearly new Mercedes gone off the cliff near Mar del Oro and who'd been driving it? Chances were good it was a stolen car and maybe the plates had been changed. He'd have to check with the local authorities.

''What do you say we get the heck out of here?'' he asked. He caught her hand.

''The sooner the better as far as I'm concerned.''

Her laughter, her smile, were infectious. As though a huge weight had been lifted from both their shoulders, they scampered back to the front of the house like two adolescents caught snooping around a haunted house.

It was too late to drive back home that evening, so

Johnny stopped at the one motel in town, a wanna-be quaint two-story building with gingerbread gables and fake tulips planted in the flower beds. After he registered at the front desk, they walked next door to a coffee shop to have dinner. The inviting outside tables with their bright yellow umbrellas were all occupied, so they went inside.

Marla slid the infant seat holding Terri into the booth and sat down beside her. Johnny took a seat opposite her. He was wearing civilian clothes today, a copper-colored sport shirt that seemed to deepen the color of his eyes and make his complexion look even more ruddy.

"I've changed my mind," she announced after she'd ordered a glass of Chardonnay from the waitress.

"You don't want wine?" Johnny asked.

"No, I do. But I've decided the past doesn't matter."

He raised his brows. "Oh?"

"I may never fully know who I am, where I was raised. Who, if anyone, I was married to."

"You were married, kitten. You aren't the kind of woman who fools around."

"Since I don't remember who I was, I could have been anything." She shivered and looked at the splashy ring on her finger, then slid it off. "For all I know, this is a zirconia I bought for myself to mislead people into believing I was married."

"It looks real enough to me. You could have it appraised."

"I don't want to. What I want is to start from where I am now and go forward." She dropped the ring into her purse, symbolically putting the past behind her and stepping out into an unknown future. "I like who I am now. I'm not so sure I liked who I was before. I may have been a snob or temperamental. Someone's doormat. Or worse. I don't know and I don't care to find out."

"If you have a husband, he deserves—"

"As you pointed out, if he exists he hasn't exactly come looking for me. That certainly sends a message, doesn't it?"

"There could be reasons."

"Johnny." Reaching across the table, she placed her hand on his. "I found something special in Mar del Oro." Including a man with whom she wanted to spend the rest of her life, a man she wanted to be the father of her child. The man whose name she'd written on her daughter's birth certificate.

"You were under a lot of stress, what with the accident and your pregnancy. You can't know—"

"I know I have friends in del Oro. Your mother. Rita and Dora. Ann and Jodie. I'd like to count you among the friends I've made."

He rubbed his thumb over hers. "More than that, Marla."

She warmed at the sincerity in his voice. It gave her hope that she wouldn't have to face a future without him—given enough time for them both to sort out their feelings for each other. "I know you were only pretending to be married to me. It had to have been an incredible sacrifice for you to make.''

Color rose to his cheeks and his lips twitched into a wry grin. ''I wouldn't exactly call it a sacrifice. Frustrating as hell when I knew I couldn't...'' He shrugged. ''You're a very beautiful woman, Marla. Sexy.''

She laughed. ''Till a month ago, I was the size of a whale and I haven't exactly gotten my figure back yet. How could you think—''

''You're the sexiest woman I've ever known. And all that time I didn't have the right to—''

''I know—my noble knight.'' She smiled back at him, squeezed his hand, grateful the sexual attraction she'd been feeling from the beginning wasn't one-sided.

''There are those who'd tell me I've been the world's biggest fool.''

''I'm not one of them, Johnny.''

The waitress returned with their wine, ready to take their orders.

When the waitress left, Marla lifted her glass. ''Here's to the future.''

Studying her intently, he touched her glass with his. ''The future.''

Shivers raced down her spine. Whatever the past had been, her focus had to be on all the tomorrows ahead of her—and her daughter. Their eyes locking over the tops of their wineglasses, they drank to all of those tomorrows.

After the sip she'd taken, smooth and slightly

sweet, Marla set her glass back on the table. "I've been thinking I'd like to do something with my interest in art."

"You're going to be a painter?"

"Well, maybe not that just yet, at least not professionally except for doing odd jobs for Dora." She wondered at the possibility she could actually paint, even lead soldiers. "I can do Dora's miniatures at home without having to leave Terri. I thought, with luck, I could find a part-time job at one of the galleries in town. Then maybe I could get my own place."

His brows lowered over his dark eyes. "You can stay with me, Marla. As long as you need to."

Something in her chest caught. She wanted him to offer more, but it was too early for that, their new relationship too fragile. In many ways, they were on unfamiliar ground. "I don't want to impose on you."

"You won't be. Besides, finding a place where you can keep Beau isn't going to be easy. You'd be better off staying with me for a while."

She hadn't thought of that. Perhaps in her other life she hadn't been a practical person who thought things through with all their ramifications. If she was on her own now, she'd have to learn to do that.

A new person, that's who she'd have to be. Considering she didn't know who she'd been before, that ought to be easy. "I'd want to pay rent—for both me and Terri."

Johnny coughed, the sip of wine he'd been taking

catching in his throat. "We can work that out," he said.

Just then, the waitress brought their salads and a basket of sourdough rolls. Marla broke one in half and took a bite. "You know, I've been so worried about who I *was,* it feels good to think about who I can become."

He smiled at her across the table. "Mama's answer to that question was 'Anything you want.' Then she'd make it pretty darn clear what we kids did with our lives had better be worthwhile."

"I hope I'll be as good a mother as yours is."

"You will be."

His confidence buoyed her. She felt freed from her unknown past, her spirit light.

All during dinner they considered possibilities for her future, each one becoming more outrageous and ranging from being hired to redecorate the White House to having her own miniatures on display at the Smithsonian. All the time, Terri slept contentedly in her car seat beside Marla, gaining the admiration of the waitress and casual passersby.

"Maybe I'll just stay at home and run for mayor of del Oro," Marla said, laughing as she drank her after-dinner coffee. "Think I'd get many votes?"

Eyes twinkling, he said, "I'm not sure I want you to be my boss."

"Why not? I'm honest, evenhanded. I'd make a good boss," she said, taking mock offense.

"I'm afraid I'd have to charge you with sexual harassment."

"Me?" she sputtered.

"I've never seen you so happy. You're glowing with it. If I wanted to make love with you before— and I did almost from the moment I met you—now you're driving me to distraction. Definitely harassing me."

"Oh, Johnny..." Her heart lodged in her throat.

"I booked us separate rooms at the motel, kitten. I didn't know—"

Reaching across the table, she linked her fingers with his. "We'll only need one room, Johnny."

"Are you sure?"

"Positive."

Chapter Ten

She came out of the bathroom after her shower wearing the sea-green nightgown Johnny had given her. Now he wished he'd bought something more feminine and lacy, more see-through. Even so, with the light behind her, he could detect the outline of her body, the curve of her hips, the way her waist nipped in and the swell of her full breasts.

His body responded with a force that shook him. He'd have to be gentle with her and that wasn't going to be easy. He wanted her almost more than life itself.

"Is Terri all right?" she asked. She'd brushed her hair and it glowed golden in the dim light. He noticed that she kept twisting her hands together.

"Not a peep since you fed her and put her down." They'd draped a blanket over the crib the motel had furnished—for a sense of privacy and to keep the light from shining in the baby's eyes.

Her gaze slid nervously to the king-size bed. Her breasts rose on a deep breath. "I meant to buy some sexy lingerie before we...when I still thought we were married. A catalogue came in the mail."

"You're sexy enough just as you are. With any luck I'll have that gown off you in milliseconds anyway. Fancy lingerie would be a waste."

She gave him a look that was near panic.

"Marla, kitten, we don't have to do this if you've changed your mind." Though it would probably kill him if he didn't get release from the tension that had been building since the night he'd found her on the beach. Never in his life had he wanted a woman so much, so fiercely. "You might not even be healed enough to—"

"I'm fine. I asked the doctor. And I definitely haven't changed my mind. But it's so odd. I know I've made love before. Or at least had sex." Smiling wryly, she glanced toward the crib in the corner of the room. "But for the life of me, I can't remember doing it. I'm not even sure how to begin."

"I do." He crossed over to her and gently took her in his arms, pressing a kiss to her forehead. "As far as I'm concerned, you're a virgin, sweetheart. I'll be that careful with you, I swear it."

"Oh, Johnny. I'm so lucky you found me."

No, he'd been the lucky one. But filled with emotion as he was, he couldn't speak. She'd taken off her wedding ring. With no known ties to the past, she was his to claim. He would show her how much he wanted her.

Bending slightly, he tasted her lips, no more than that, and he felt a shudder ripple through her. "You don't remember kissing?"

"Only your kisses. The first one that day in the

hospital was so special. I liked it, probably more than I should have.''

''That's definitely a step in the right direction. We'll build memories together. Starting now.'' He deepened the kiss, relishing her innocent response as her tongue teased hesitantly with his. She tasted of mint and smelled of fresh floral soap. He inhaled, memorizing her scent. ''Where do you suppose you like to be kissed best?''

''I don't...'' Her voice caught as he moved from her sweet-tasting mouth to the column of her neck.

''I like kissing you here.'' He nibbled gently. ''Does it feel good?''

''Oh, yes.'' Tilting her head to give him easier access, she sighed. ''You're very good at this, aren't you?''

''I want to hear you purr, kitten.''

''I'm not sure...'' He moved his lips to her ear. She moaned softly.

''That's right. Your first time is going to be special, sweetheart. I promise.''

Her arms were around his neck, her body pressing against his. At every point where they touched, where their bodies connected, he was on fire, hot and hard. Her breasts. Her pelvis. The length of her legs against his. He gritted his teeth. Never had he been called upon to stay so tightly in control. The burden of bringing her pleasure this first time weighed as heavily on his conscience as it would if she'd truly been a virgin. For him, that's what she was. No matter what it took, he wouldn't fail her.

His palm skimmed up her midriff to graze the side of her breast. She drew in a breath.

"Does that hurt?"

"No, I'm just a little sensitive is all."

"And beautiful." The fullness of her breasts fascinated him. More than anything, he wanted to feel their weight in his hand, see the fine veins on her pale skin. Tentatively, he flicked his thumb across her nipple. "How does that feel?"

She shuddered. "Like heaven. I've wanted you to touch me. For so long…"

He bent his head to her breast, found her nipple and tugged gently through the cloth that covered it. "I envy Terri."

Clasping her hands around his head, she pulled him closer and moaned. "Don't envy her. This is different. Much different."

"I should hope so."

"Johnny?" Her breath caught.

"Hmm?" He laved her again.

"Do you suppose we could lie down? My legs… Oh, my…" She collapsed against him.

"Whatever you'd like." Scooping her into his arms, he carried her the few steps to the bed and laid her down. His arms still wrapped around her, he settled next to her. "Can you tell me what you like?"

"No. Yes. Everything. Kiss me some more, Johnny."

"My pleasure." With great patience, he kissed her everywhere he could—her face, her arms, her fingertips. Slowly, with great care, until she moaned aloud and twisted against him.

"More, Johnny. It's not enough."

"I'm doing the very best I can." And he was hurting, aching so much to fully take her. But he wanted her ready; he didn't want to cause her any pain.

Finally, he slipped her nightgown up over her hips and then over her head, revealing the triangle of natural blond hair at the apex of her thighs and her milk-swollen breasts. "I've never known a more beautiful woman." He covered her with kisses, nuzzling between her breasts, traveling the fine line from her belly button to her most sensitive regions.

Her hands tugged at his shirt, pulling it loose from his trousers. "Too many clothes," she murmured. "Not fair."

She was right. His clothes had to go. They ended up in a heap on the floor beside the bed.

Her hands caressing him were like fiery butterflies brushing their wings against his skin—his chest, his shoulders, the nape of his neck—exploring first one spot and then another. He wanted to capture her but was afraid of hurting her.

Her uninhibited passion astounded him, the way she gave herself over to him, trusting him. "Kitten, kitten, you taste so good."

"I want more of you, Johnny." Her breathing was close to a sob. "More than kisses."

He was helpless to resist her plea. Positioning himself between her legs, he whispered, "If it hurts even a little, tell me. I'll stop. I swear."

In the light from the far end of the room, he saw her smile. "There's no way I'm going to let you stop." She lifted her hips to him. "Ever."

Cautiously, he eased himself forward to explore her most tender terrain. He wouldn't let her rush him into hurting her though his restraint was causing every muscle in his body to tense. Slowly...

"Johnny?" She arched. "Oh, please..."

He watched her expression as he slipped into her moist heat. Her eyes widened, but not in pain. He pulled out and entered her again, this time more deeply.

"Yes," she said on a breathless sigh. "So good..."

"Good" did not begin to describe how she felt to Johnny. He was a part of her and she of him, a perfect match. She lifted her legs, inviting him deeper, and he began a slow rhythm that made his breath come hard and fast.

"Kitten, I'm not sure how long—"

"Don't hold back. Don't..." She sobbed a low, helpless sound.

He stifled her cry with his mouth and felt her coming apart in his arms as she drew from him all that he had to give. Pleasure speared through him; tiny red lights flashed behind his closed eyelids. His release was more powerful than anything he had ever known. More complete. And as he felt her continuing shudders closing around him, Johnny knew a joy he'd never truly expected to experience.

Marla, the woman who'd appeared from out of the sea mist, was his.

As she lay in Johnny's arms, her body still pulsing, her breathing slowly returning to normal, Marla knew she had experienced death and rebirth. The future stretched out before her in glorious shades of red and orange like a summer sunrise. Her chest expanded with the beauty of it all.

Johnny. Her gentle knight to whom she'd given her heart. Her flesh-and-blood talisman, her good-luck charm, even better than a lead figurine sitting motionless on the mantel. And much more satisfying, she thought with a sleepy smile.

At that moment, nothing in the universe had the power to dampen her hopes, her dreams. A magical triangle bonded her and Johnny and Terri together. The attachment was strong, unbreakable, forged when he'd rescued her on the beach and tempered when he'd held Terri in his hands at the moment of her birth.

They were a family, unofficial now, but Marla had no doubt that time would rectify that minor inconsistency. At the heart of it all, they belonged together.

At three o'clock, when Terri woke for her feeding, Johnny brought her into bed with them, holding Marla as she nursed the baby.

"When do they sleep through the night?" he asked.

"At about six weeks, if we're lucky."

"That's too bad. I was hoping it was longer."

She shot him a surprised look. "Why on earth would you want her to keep waking us up in the middle of the night?"

"Because now that we're both awake, I figure when she goes back to sleep we can make love again. It's an opportunity I wouldn't want to miss."

And he didn't, not that night at any rate. And Marla discovered she liked the idea of waking every night to make love with Johnny—a part of the happiness she was building into her future.

"YOU WANT TO MAKE a leisurely ride of it and take Highway 1, or would you rather take the inland route again?"

"I definitely want to get back home to del Oro by the quickest route possible." Strangely, Marla didn't feel in the least embarrassed about having made love with Johnny last night—twice—although she was a little tender. They'd been living together for six weeks. Becoming intimate seemed the most natural thing in the world. Until he'd told her otherwise, she'd thought of him as her husband. In her heart, she still did.

"Okay. Fine by me." Smiling at her across the room, he tucked his shirt into his pants. "We'll catch some breakfast next door and then be on our way."

With all the baby paraphernalia, it took them a little extra time to pack up and load the car. The day promised to be another sunny one, however, and Marla's spirits were high.

A couple was just leaving one of the outdoor tables as they arrived at the coffee shop. When the table was cleared, Johnny asked the hostess to seat them there, then he tilted the umbrella to shade Terri's eyes. A low wall of painted white bricks separated the tables from the pedestrians walking and jogging along the sidewalk.

"This wouldn't be a bad place to live," Marla commented. The air was fresh with just a trace of the ocean that wasn't too many miles away, and the little village looked prosperous but not at all touristy, the shops catering to the wealthy who lived in the area.

"It's a bit upscale for my pocketbook," Johnny admitted. "My house, if I owned it free and clear, which I don't, probably wouldn't make a down payment on any of those houses we saw yesterday."

She laughed. "Those weren't houses, Johnny. They were estates."

"Like I said, a bit pricey for me."

When the waitress arrived, he ordered eggs sunny-side up, sausages, hash browns, toast and orange juice. Marla, reveling in the knowledge that a nursing mother could safely consume extra calories without paying the price around her waist, ordered French toast and bacon.

"We both must have worked up an appetite last night," Johnny said, his patented smile filled with memories.

Heat stole up her neck to flush her cheeks. "You'll get no argument from me about that," she replied softly for his ears only. "You are one accomplished lover."

"You're pretty good yourself, kitten." He reached across the table to take her hand.

"Victoria? Victoria Stapleton? Darling, whatever are you doing back in town?"

Marla's head snapped up. The woman standing on

the opposite side of the low wall was decked out in
a designer warm-up suit, though she didn't look the
type who ever broke a sweat. Expensive teardrop earrings dangled from her ears, gold bracelets clinked
when she moved, and her lapel pin could have been
an authentic Tiffany piece.

Her stomach churning on the cup of coffee she'd
consumed, Marla stared in horrible fascination at the
stranger, who wasn't a stranger at all.

"And that baby!" the woman continued to gush.
"My goodness, let me get a closer look at her. Why
she's just the spittin' image of that no-good husband
of yours. What a pity. I bet you wished—"

"Excuse me, ma'am." Johnny stood. "I gather you
know this woman?" He gestured across the table at
Marla.

Her perfectly smooth forehead, stretched taut by
more than one face-lift, creased. "Why, sugar, of
course I know Victoria. Didn't we just co-chair almost every Assistance League fund-raiser for the past
umpteen years? And didn't she and I win, I mean
really win, the medal-play women's charity golf tournament at the country club last year?" She gave him
an assessing look and her pencil-thin brows rose suggestively. "I must say, Victoria, your taste in men
has improved enormously since you planted that son
of a bee husband of yours. More power to you, I
always say."

All the color drained from Marla's face and she felt
faint.

Dear God in heaven! She *was* Victoria Stapleton.

Chapter Eleven

"Ma'am, would you mind joining us for breakfast?" Using his most nonthreatening voice, Johnny gestured toward the empty chair at the table. He could tell from the way Marla had turned so pale, she wasn't going to be able to speak any time soon. And a lot of questions needed to be asked—and answered. "Or a cup of coffee?"

"I do wish you wouldn't call me ma'am. It makes me feel absolutely ancient." She practically fluttered her mascara-coated lashes at him, though her thick coat of makeup didn't cover the fact she was on the downhill side of fifty and could have already hit the speed bump of sixty.

"Yes, ma'am. And your name is?"

"Why, I'm Adele Forsythe. Victoria will tell you that." Growing agitated, she glanced at Marla, or Victoria as she called her. "What's going on, darling? Who is this man?"

Johnny hated to do it, but with Marla still silenced by shock, he produced his police ID. "If you'll just sit down, Ms. Forsythe, there are a few questions I'd like to ask you.''

Warily, she walked around to the opening in the low brick wall, returning to settle in the chair opposite Marla. ''My darling, are you in trouble with the law?'' The question came out in a shocked whisper.

Marla managed to shake her head. ''Adele...I had an accident.''

''Your friend...'' He wanted to call her Marla, but Adele Forsythe wouldn't know her by that name. Johnny didn't know her as Victoria. ''She had an injury that resulted in amnesia. We're here hoping she might recover her memory.''

''Oh, you poor, poor dear. Tell me if there's anything I can do.''

Johnny could almost see Adele's eyes light up at the opportunity to help...and then pass on the gossip she gleaned at the next Assistance League meeting.

''We went by the address on Oak Terrace we had for the Stapleton home and actually peeked inside. Mar—uh, Victoria didn't recognize the interior.'' His gut twisted as he realized he'd have to start thinking of her as Victoria, a woman who lived in a ten-thousand-square-foot house with a damn four-car garage. Hell, he was lucky to get his one car, a compact, into his garage.

''Oh, she wouldn't, my goodness, no.'' She waved her hand as if chasing a pesky gnat away from her face. ''That new family, the Ruwadis, are simply too gauche, don't you know? Since you sold them the house, they've redecorated everything, and without an ounce of class. Such a shame." She lifted a single shoulder. "They're definitely not Marin County, if you know what I mean."

Johnny certainly got the point. The son of a migrant farmworker wasn't exactly Marin County, either, not the country-club set anyway.

"I sold the house?" Marla asked in a lackluster tone.

"Of course you did. Who'd want to live in that ol' place after you found out what your husband had done. I know I wouldn't."

The waitress came with their orders, setting the plates in front of Johnny and Marla. "Can I get you something, honey?" she asked the new arrival.

"Just coffee, no cream. Well, maybe an English muffin, if that's all right? Whole wheat?" She checked with Johnny.

"Fine." As far as he was concerned, Adele could have his whole breakfast. He suspected Marla had lost her appetite, too.

Struggling out of the shock that had left her numb, Marla managed to ask, "What awful thing did my husband do?" A thousand fragments of memory began to dart through her brain in a disjointed collage. An Author's Day she and Adele had organized to raise money for a health clinic that served indigents. A golf tournament for the Alzheimer's Foundation. Driving into the city—San Francisco—for a Children's Hospital Auxiliary event. The Fine Arts Gallery. All worthy causes, yet her life had seemed empty. A handsome husband who was so slick she hadn't guessed he was betraying her.

"Darling, the wife is always the last to know, isn't that what they say? We all thought you knew, truly we did, and that you chose to look the other way. So many of us prefer being pragmatic rather than losing our comfortable lives over nothing worth mentioning. Like sex." She winked her heavily mascaraed eye. "We just assumed you felt that way, too."

She stared at the older woman, not a friend exactly. More like a fellow employee you had to be leery of for fear every word you spoke would get back to the boss. Yes, she remembered Adele Forsythe and not with a great deal of fondness. But in the social world of Marin County, she was a powerful person, one David Stapleton had wanted his wife to court. And she'd done as he asked.

"David was unfaithful to me?" His name tasted sour on her tongue, as though she'd dredged up a bitter memory that was better left buried.

"Oh, worse than that, darling." Adele leaned back while the waitress placed a cup in front of her and poured the coffee. "He'd had a lover for years, a tart he picked up at some bar in the city ages ago. Not exactly what I'd call a casual affair. And absolutely no class. Dreadful woman. Cheap, if you know what I mean."

Humiliation swept through Marla, who was unable to think of herself as Victoria even though she now knew that's who she was. Adele Forsythe had known and not told her of David's affair. Marla had naively assumed the problems in her marriage were all her fault, the result of her inability to love a man fully. *Loosen up, Victoria. You're as frigid as the iceberg that sank the Titanic,* David had told her.

Shuddering at the insult, she shot a glance at Johnny. Dammit all! She *was* capable of love, a deep, all-consuming love. And she sure as hell wasn't frigid. She'd proved that to her satisfaction—and Johnny's—last night. If there had been anything wrong in her marriage, it was David's fault, not hers.

"You said something about…planting David?" Marla asked, stubbornly refusing to think of herself as Victoria. "What happened?"

Adele gave a loose-wristed wave of her hand. "He wrapped himself and that bimbo of his around a telephone pole one night. The police report said his blood-alcohol level was practically a two, and hers wasn't much better. They'd been celebrating, I guess."

"Celebrating what?"

"Lord, I don't know. He'd probably made a financial killing. He was really good at his business. At least according to my Edward, he was."

Marla hadn't eaten a bite of her breakfast and neither had Johnny. In fact, the smell of bacon was making her nauseous. Adele, however, vigorously spread her English muffin with butter the moment it was delivered, then scooped jelly from the tiny plastic container onto it, as well. She bit into the muffin with relish.

"Of course, there have been rumors," Adele said after devouring the first bite.

"Rumors about what?" Johnny asked.

She lifted her bony shoulders. "David was an investment counselor, the heir apparent after your father died," she said to Marla. "He'd taken over the firm. With your blessing, I assume. My Edward suspected David didn't necessarily share your father's sense of ethics."

The memory cells in Marla's head made a painful shift from David to her father, Robert Tolliver. A stern-faced man, he rarely smiled and never issued a single word of praise no matter how hard she tried to please him. *She didn't belong. She wasn't his child.* She'd heard those words as a child. Her parents had been behind closed doors, but their voices had risen in a crescendo of anger—anger that flayed her with guilt. They were arguing over her. *We never should have adopted her,* he said with cruel dismissal.

Marla could barely draw a breath as the memory engulfed her. She hadn't been wanted. Not by her father. Certainly not by her biological mother who'd given her away. In all these years, she'd found no one who could love her.

Except Johnny. And he'd only been pretending.

In her infant seat, Terri began to squirm, making little sounds of discomfort. Marla unbuckled the safety belt and snatched her baby up in her arms.

Her chest heaved. She didn't give a damn about David Stapleton. Or Adele. She had a child to love.

"I have to feed her," she said almost frantically.

She wanted to get away from this place, away from the memories. David had betrayed her. Or perhaps she'd betrayed herself by marrying a man her father had selected for her. *The heir apparent.*

Her memories coalesced into a painful knot in her chest, and she stood. Her throat burned; her muscles ached as if she had the flu. She'd sold the firm—her father's company and David's toy—for a song before her former husband's grave had settled in the ground. She'd wanted none of it. Hated all it represented.

"I want to go now, Johnny," she said.

"Right." He came to his feet, too, fishing his wallet out of his pocket, tossing cash on the table.

"Aren't you going to eat your French toast?" Adele asked. Her pale blue eyes darted from Marla to Johnny and back again. "You don't look well, darling. Is there something I can…?"

Marla didn't wait to hear the rest of Adele's question. Carrying her baby, she marched away from the coffee shop like a cowardly soldier in desperate retreat. She couldn't escape fast enough.

Johnny grabbed the infant seat with one hand and hurried after her. He caught up with her before she reached his car and snared her by the arm. "Slow down, kitten." She was running scared, panic in her eyes. He was afraid she'd do something foolish, like run away from him.

"I want to go home."

"I'll take you wherever you want to go. But let's stop and think a minute."

"I don't want to think. I just want to go."

"You're remembering?"

"Yes. No. Oh, God, it was so awful."

She was fighting to stay on a razor edge of control, using all the inner strength Johnny had observed not to slip into hysteria. He wanted to take care of her, to make up for her slug of a husband who'd been running around on her. Damn! The jerk must have been dim-witted not to know what he was missing.

"Come on, I haven't checked out of the room yet." He ushered her that direction. "We'll go back inside, try to calm down. You've had a shock."

"That's an understatement." Her brittle laugh nearly broke his heart. "The real shocker was the night two police officers showed up at my door to announce that David was dead, and did I just happen to know the woman in the car with him? The woman, it turned out, who'd been his mistress since before we were married."

Juggling the infant seat, Johnny unlocked the door to their motel room and shoved it open so Marla could go inside. The bed was still unmade, the bedding a jumble from their night of making love. He wanted to take her back to bed right now, soothe her and tell her everything was going to be all right. But he couldn't do that. Not now with the baby demanding to be fed. And maybe never again.

"I was such a naive fool, I never even suspected. Not even when he kept putting me off about starting a family. He didn't want me to get pregnant." Distractedly, she sat at the table in the corner of the room and opened her blouse so Terri could nurse. "Meanwhile, everyone else knew what he was up to. As soon as I sold the house, I left. I couldn't wait to get out of this town.''

"You must have had friends here.''

"Acquaintances, that's all they were. People who wanted me to write a fat check for their favorite charity. Friends would've told me what was going on, not talked about me behind my back.'' She released her breast and Terri latched onto the nipple. "Poor little Victoria,'' she said in a mocking tone. "Too dumb to know what a gigolo she'd married. All he'd wanted was my money—and my father's connections and good name. David made me believe he loved me. What a fool I was.''

Johnny tried to drag his gaze away from the intimate picture of Marla and her baby. He couldn't. He sat down on the edge of the bed near her, rested his forearms on his thighs and linked his fingers together, wishing he could hold her. Suddenly, he was self-conscious about who he was and where he'd come from—a strawberry picker from Oxnard who didn't belong in upscale Marin County.

"So you were in the process of moving when you had your accident?''

For a thoughtful moment, some of the fury went out of her eyes. "I'd bought a house in San Luis Obispo. I was going to...'' For the first time since Adele had spotted them, Marla smiled, although only faintly. "I was going to finish my degree in art history that I'd started a long time ago. My father had insisted I switch to a business major—something useful, he said—as if he ever would have let me have anything to do with his company.''

''Are your parents still living?''

''No. Mother was in her late forties and Dad more than fifty when they adopted me—against his better judgment, I learned as I was growing up. He died of a heart attack about four years ago.'' She blinked back the tears that suddenly pooled in her eyes. ''A year later, Mother died in a ski lodge in the Alps. An avalanche.''

''I'm sorry, kitten.''

She shrugged. ''They weren't very emotional people, either of them. Almost cold.'' Idly, she stroked Terri's head and ran the back of her fingers along the baby's cheek.

It was easy to guess that Marla had needed a lot more love than her parents had been willing or able to give her. Evidently, her husband hadn't been much better in that department. Johnny was almost sorry the creep was already dead. He'd like to make David Stapleton pay for all the pain he'd caused Marla.

''So the reason no one reported you missing was because you'd already said your goodbyes here in Marin—''

''Such as they were.''

''And you hadn't yet moved into your new place.''

''The Realtor in San Luis Obispo must wonder what on earth happened to me. My obstetrician, too, for that matter. I was supposed to be signing the final escrow papers the day after my accident. The money had already been transferred from my bank here to the escrow company. I was paying cash.''

Johnny couldn't stop himself from wondering how much cash she was talking about. Probably a helluva lot more than the twenty percent he'd put down on his place. ''Maybe before we leave we ought to check with your bank to see what happened.''

''Yes. I can check my other accounts, too.''

Accounts? As in plural? Not that Johnny doubted she was worth megabucks. He had suspected as much all along and known that would put her out of his league.

Terri had gone lax in Marla's arms, her tiny hand resting on her breast. She slipped the nipple free.

Johnny did his best not to think about how he had kissed her just as intimately last night as they made love. His efforts to block the thought weren't good enough, so he got up and walked around the room to the far side of the bed.

''My middle name is Caitlin,'' she said softly. He could almost see the painful memories radiating from her like waves of heat on a scorching summer day. ''When I was little, I used to pretend I was a girl named Caitlin, whom everyone loved. I could dance and sing and was the smartest, prettiest girl in school. My father and mother loved me more than any other little girl was loved in the whole world. I never got yelled at. I never disappointed them by being stupid or clumsy or saying the wrong thing. I used to think if I could really be that Caitlin, I'd be happy. But no matter how hard I pretended, I never could be her.''

God, she was breaking his heart. That she had survived at all with so little affection spoke volumes
about her inner strength.

"Maybe that's why I lost my memory." She
looked up at him, her eyes glistening with unshed
tears like the sun glinting off a green sea. "I've always *wanted* to be someone else. For a little while, I
was."

His voice thick with emotion, he said, "As far as
I'm concerned, who you are right now is perfect."

"It may not be very nice to speak ill of the dead,
but I'm glad David is gone. It's given me a chance
to start over."

But start over where? Johnny wondered. In a big
fancy house in San Luis Obispo that she paid for with
cash? With shopping trips to New York and London
in her spare time, and art galleries thrown in for good
measure? Now that she had her memory back, no way
would she be satisfied in a bungalow with an ocean
view if she had as much money as he suspected.

A man should be able to support his woman in the
way she was used to.

In Marla's case, he couldn't do that. And in spite
of what she'd said, he was sure she'd slip away to be
that woman she used to be—Victoria Stapleton. She
deserved the very best. Not a migrant worker's son
who'd been twenty-five years old before he figured
out which fork to use at a formal dinner. And even
then, he still sometimes got it wrong.

THE BANK MANAGER STOOD the moment he saw her,
as she'd known he would. The Stapleton accounts

were substantial, as had been the Tolliver holdings. Her money had given her status in Marin County. In San Luis Obispo, she'd intended to keep a low profile.

"Mrs. Stapleton, what a pleasure to see you."

She could no longer pretend to be someone else. "Hello, Damien. How have you been?" She extended her hand for a brief handshake just the way her mother had taught her to do so many years ago and so many lessons in etiquette past. His gaze flicked toward Johnny. She hesitated a moment, wondering how to introduce him. No easy label came to mind. *Friend* seemed inadequate, but except for one night, he wasn't her lover, either, not that she'd share that part of their relationship with a bank manager. A week ago, she would have called Johnny her husband, but that had never been true. They'd both been pretending. "I'd like you to meet John Fuentes of Mar del Oro. Damien Vincente."

They exchanged handshakes and pleasantries, Johnny surpassing the bank manager in both physique and the ability to command respect, even though he was dressed casually in slacks and a sport shirt.

"And I see your little bundle of joy has arrived," Damien cooed like a politician seeking votes, although somewhat nervously. "Such a pretty little thing. What a pleasure she must be to you after the untimely loss of your husband."

Stiffening, Victoria shifted Terri to her other shoulder. "I wonder if I could check my accounts? And

I've lost my ATM card as well as my checkbook. Perhaps you could arrange replacements?''

He blinked, his Adam's apple fluttering. ''But of course. It would be my pleasure.''

If he got any more ''pleasure'' out of her visit, Victoria thought she might gag on it. ''Thank you. You're most kind.''

With a broad gesture of his arm, like a maître d' at a high-class restaurant ushering guests to their table, he indicated they could wait in the chairs at his desk. Long teller lines weren't necessary for those with financial clout.

''I do hope, Mrs. Stapleton, that matters have, ah, run smoothly for you since your move? Nothing untoward, I trust?''

She frowned at his odd question. Unwilling to discuss her personal affairs with him, she replied, ''My relocation has gone quite smoothly, thank you.''

''I'm, er, pleased to hear that.'' He bowed deferentially. His hand trembled slightly. ''This won't take but a minute. I'll have someone bring you coffee, if you'd like.''

''No, we're fine.'' She waved him off.

Johnny held out the chair for her. ''Tell me more about your husband's life.''

She looked up at him. ''As Adele said, he was an investment counselor, mostly venture-capital projects.''

''Stocks and bonds?''

''The firm didn't have a seat on the New York Stock Exchange, if that's what you're asking. But they did deal in stocks. Mostly start-up companies, which are pretty risky. Father had a real flair for picking out winners.''

"And your late husband? Was he just as talented?"

She glanced away. "David didn't discuss business with me." After the first few months of their marriage, he hadn't discussed much of anything with her.

She'd wasted seven years of her life on David Stapleton. She'd have been better off to get her art degree. As it was, she'd made some darn good investments in the works of unknown artists who'd grown in prestige. Her success in identifying budding young talent was nothing to sneer at, though neither her father nor her husband had thought a bit of paint dabbed on canvas worth their time or energy. She knew better.

Damien returned just as Terri began to fuss. Johnny took the baby from her so her hands would be free to sign the necessary papers for a new ATM card. As he jiggled Terri in his lap, Victoria was struck once again with what a natural father he was, able to give love as easily as drawing a breath.

Dear heaven, she wished Johnny were the father of her child, the man to whom she could turn to allay her fears. A man who could love her unconditionally. She couldn't pretend to be his wife any longer. It wasn't fair to him.

After all he'd done for her, meant to her, they had to start over. Deep in her soul, she was afraid the woman she'd once been wasn't worthy of Johnny. And she wasn't sure the new person she'd become was enough for a man as elementally masculine, as thoroughly good, as her Johnny.

The bank manager returned with her new ATM card and printouts of her accounts. Her other financial records were in storage in San Luis Obispo. There'd be plenty of time to get them later. Right now, she just wanted to go home...with Johnny.

"YOU WANT TO SWING BY your new place?" Johnny asked as they approached San Luis Obispo on U.S. 101 late that afternoon. The summer sun slanted in the passenger window at a low angle, and the traffic flowed at a steady seventy-plus miles per hour, every driver liable for a speeding ticket if a cop happened along, even Johnny.

Victoria stretched, bone weary from being in the car so long. "Frankly, I'm exhausted and I suspect Terri's going to start getting fussy any minute now. The new house can wait."

"You'll be wanting to move in pretty soon, I imagine."

"I'm in no particular rush." She'd prefer to stay at Johnny's house indefinitely, but he hadn't exactly extended the invitation.

"I can check with the DMV to get you a new driver's license. You'll probably want to buy a car, too."

She frowned. "I suppose so."

"There's a fair-size Mercedes dealership in San Luis. You might be able to get something decent right off the showroom floor. I don't know what kind of deals they make.''

"I may not want a Mercedes this time.''

He slanted her a glance. "There's a Cadillac dealership, too.''

"I don't need to have the most expensive car in town, Johnny.''

"I figured you'd want something nice. You can afford it ''

"Yes, I can. But that doesn't mean I have to spend money simply because it's there.'' On the contrary, she'd just as soon no one knew the extent of her wealth. Up to now, money had brought her nothing but trouble.

"Whatever.'' He shrugged, slowing as the traffic became heavier near the freeway exit that led to the college campus and cars jockeyed for position.

"Are you having a problem with my being well-off financially?'' she asked.

"Not me. I'm happy for you.''

He didn't look happy. If anything, he'd seemed particularly tense ever since they left the bank in Marin County, a tightness around his mouth, his brows lowered. Even when they stopped for a quick drive-through lunch, they'd hardly spoken a word beyond necessary conversation.

"Money has never been particularly important to me, Johnny.''

"That's because you've always had plenty.''

"I didn't have a dime when you found me on the beach. And I didn't miss having it.''

"You thought we were married."

"Yes, I know." Those few weeks while she believed she was married to Johnny had been the happiest time of her life.

"I was supporting you."

The undercurrents of this conversation were making her seriously uncomfortable. "Would you like me to pay you back?"

He swore under his breath. "No, that's not what I want."

"Then what? You're as grouchy as a porcupine who's had his skin turned inside out. What's going on?"

Turning onto the highway that led to Mar del Oro, he flipped down the sun visor. In spite of his sunglasses, deep lines appeared at the corners of his eyes as he squinted through the windshield. "How long do you figure it will take you to move into your new place?"

A sinking feeling filled her stomach and threatened to close her throat. He was deliberately ignoring her question. David had done much the same when she pressed for better communication. So had her father. To both of them she had been little more than a lamppost, someone to be ignored until they had a need for her—and then she was expected to perform properly.

Struggling to control her quivering chin, she said, "I'll be ready to move in a week or so. There's some painting I wanted to get done, new carpeting to be installed. Eventually, I want to remodel the kitchen and bathrooms.'' But none of that seemed to matter now.

He nodded stiffly. "Great. When you're ready, I'll help you get settled.''

A band tightened around Victoria's chest. He wanted her out of his life as fast as possible. She'd hoped they'd have a little more time together, time enough to explore their new relationship.

Obviously, from his perspective, they didn't have a new relationship. All they had was the old one based on pretense and a single night of memories.

She gritted her teeth. Dammit! That wasn't enough. She had one week to forge a new bond with Johnny, one that would last for another fifty years or more. And she totally lacked the experience to know how to go about forming that kind of relationship. Her one effort with David had been a bust.

She vowed to do better this time.

Chapter Twelve

One week. Maybe a few days longer than that.

Johnny swore, slamming on the brakes to avoid a car that had cut him off. How was he going to keep his hands off her for that many days, that many hours?

How was he going to live without her?

He was already beginning to sweat. Every time he glanced in her direction, he thought about the night they'd spent together and how he wanted to spend another thousand nights doing the same thing. When she swept her long blond hair back from her face, he remembered how her delicate hands had caressed him with the innocent passion of an untutored lover, arousing him almost beyond endurance. When she licked her lips against the drying sun, he remembered their flavor, their soft texture.

His groin ached with the need to have her again.

His heart ached to have her always.

She was out of his league.

Damn! He wished those scuba divers had never found that car; he wished he'd never taken Marla—Victoria—back to Marin. He wished things had stayed as they were, and that wasn't fair to her...or to him.

She had goals and dreams she was now free to pursue. He couldn't hold her back. She'd been well en route to establishing a new life for herself. With all her money, she could do anything she liked.

Once in L.A., he'd been moonlighting as security for a fancy party with Hollywood stars and debutantes in attendance, the crème de la crème of society. Wealthy people like Marla, all dressed to the nines, diamonds sparkling. A blonde had latched onto him that night. She'd been so sexy, he nearly drooled. She'd had more cleavage than any woman had a right to. She'd trapped him in a dark corner, rubbed up against him real good till he had trouble remembering he was on the job.

Then she'd laughed, a shrieking sound that mocked him. "I love to make it with peasants," she'd said. "They're always so carnal!"

She'd strutted away, her hips swaying in her skin-tight dress, and Johnny had hated himself for not recognizing that she'd been toying with him the way a cat toys with a mouse.

Even on the LAPD, he'd often been a second-class citizen. A "beaner" to more than a few of his fellow officers. Someone who'd gotten there because of affirmative action. Beneath them.

Back in his high school days, he'd known enough to watch his step. He'd never so much as flirted with Ann Forrester. In spite of her being friendly, he kept his distance from the daughter of the local bank president.

Life hadn't changed all that much for a guy whose parents picked fruit and scrubbed toilets for a living.

He wasn't in Victoria's league.

"I guess you'll be glad to get your own things out of storage and have something to wear besides those cheap clothes my sister loaned you," he said tautly.

Her head whipped around and she looked stunned. "Rita's clothes have been fine. I've really appreciated her help. Frankly, I'll be happy if my old things fit again. I have the feeling my figure isn't quite back to what it was."

"Your figure's fine."

"Thank you," she said with a forced smile. "I wish I could say the same for your mood."

His frustration was so deep and painful, he nearly snarled at her. "I'm in a great mood."

Who was he kidding? Not Victoria. And certainly not himself.

WHEN HE ARRIVED at his house, the sun was a red ball low on the water, Rita's car was parked in the driveway, and Terri was squalling in the back seat. He pulled up at the curb.

"I'd better feed her in a hurry," Victoria said. She got out of the car and opened the back door, cooing to the baby in an effort to quiet her as she undid the car-seat straps and picked her up. "Mommy's here, little muffin. Oh, heavens! You're soaked through."

Beau bounded out from the back of the house, followed by Rita's three kids, then Rita herself. The dog raced for the car, his tail going about a dozen wags per second.

"Uncle Johnny! Uncle Johnny!" the children shouted in unison.

Johnny leaned his head back and took a deep breath. He wasn't up for a family reunion just at the moment.

"Hey, you two," Rita said, "when I called and got no answer, I figured I'd better feed the dog again just in case you decided to stay another night. How'd it go up north?"

Victoria waved. "Ask Johnny. I've got a starving, sopping-wet baby on my hands. I'll see you in a few minutes." She vanished into the house.

Rita halted beside the car. "Well?"

"Well what?"

"Is Marla that woman you thought she was?"

"She's Victoria Stapleton, active member of the Marin County Assistance League, local benefactress for half the charities in the county. As near as I can tell, she's got more money than Bill Gates." He'd caught a glimpse of some of the account records the bank manager had given her. The bottom lines had added up to a helluva lot.

"No fooling? I thought maybe she came from money. After her amnesia and all, she must feel like she just won the lottery."

He shoved open the car door, forcing his sister to step back. The kids were wrestling with Beau on the front lawn, a tiny patch of green compared to the expansive one at the house Victoria had sold—for cash.

"Does she have a husband?"

Trust his sister to get to the nitty-gritty. "No. She's widowed."

"Thank goodness. Well, I didn't mean it quite like that, but at least she's available—"

"She's not available to me." He went to the back of the car and popped the trunk.

"What do you mean by that?"

He yanked the suitcases out. "Have you forgotten where we come from, Sis? Strawberry fields, that's where."

"So?"

"So if we look like migrants and talk like migrants—"

"Oh, for heaven's sake, Johnny! You haven't done farmwork in a hundred years. You're the chief of police! You've got a college degree."

Slamming the trunk closed, he shoved past her. "I've still got dirt under my fingernails. The kind that never goes away."

Rita gasped. "Did she say that?"

"She didn't have to."

He felt his sister's eyes on him as he walked into the house. She hadn't married out of their class. Her husband, Rudy, had plucked a few tomatoes himself. Now he had a decent job as manager of the local drugstore and was a good provider, husband and father. Rita hadn't tried to reach beyond her roots. She hadn't been slapped back into her rightful place.

For which he was grateful, he reflected. He liked Rita and all his sisters just as they were. None of them put on airs.

But neither did Marla, he realized, frowning. He could almost hear his sister calling him a jerk for worrying about their past, but he couldn't shake the feeling he wasn't good enough for Marla...Victoria.

Federal Building, San Francisco

IT WAS AFTER HOURS so Tommy Tompkins called the prosecutor at home. He'd been out of the office all day and hadn't gotten his messages until late.

"The bank manager called—she showed up," he said with little preamble.

In the background, he heard a youngster shout, "Mom, I can't find my beach towel for tomorrow."

"Look in the dryer," the prosecutor said in an aside. "She try to withdraw her funds?"

Tommy had never pictured the prosecutor as a mother, and he wondered if he should rethink his view of the woman. Maybe outside the office she actually had a heart. "Only a couple of hundred dollars. The good news is that the bank manager got the plate number of the car she was in."

"I'll be sure to send him a gold star. Was it a rental?"

"Nope. And you won't believe who the registered owner is."

VICTORIA CAME OUT of the bedroom carrying Terri, now fed and changed and in much better spirits than she'd been a half hour ago. So was Victoria, buoyed by being back where she belonged. "Where's Rita?"

"She took the kids home."

Kneeling, Victoria spread a blanket on the floor and laid Terri down for a little playtime. The baby kicked her legs while her fists found her mouth. Victoria smiled at her, love filling her heart. What a precious gift she was.

"I thought Rita would want to hear more about what happened in Marin," she said to Johnny.

"I told her."

Standing in the kitchen, he popped the top on a beer can, the one can that had been in the refrigerator since the day he'd brought Victoria home. He wasn't exactly a drinking man. Evidently, he thought he needed one today, and something about the way he stood staring out the window at the darkening ocean gave her a sense of dread.

Hesitantly, she stood. "Do you want to talk about what's bothering you?"

"What's to talk about? You got your memory back. I'm happy for you."

Victoria didn't think so.

She crossed the room and stood behind him. She felt awkward and unsure of herself, but she couldn't *not* touch him. They'd made love. Although they weren't husband and wife, their shared intimacy meant something. Or it should have.

She slid her arms around his waist and rested her

head on his shoulder. He stiffened. Her heart tumbled in despair.

"I have a lot to thank you for." Her words were no more than a whisper. "Taking me in the way you did. Going along with the pretense that we were married."

"All part of the job."

That hurt...deeply. "You mean you'd pretend to be married to any woman who just happened along?"

"You were in trouble." He lifted his shoulders as if he could shrug her off.

She didn't intend to back away that easily. "If it means anything to you, I liked being your wife."

He swallowed some beer, the sound audible, but he didn't speak. His fine, strong body seemed encapsulated in a rigid layer of concrete so thick she couldn't break through it to find his heart. Or maybe she simply didn't know how.

"I liked making love to you last night." She wanted to make love with him again tonight and all the tomorrows they'd toasted to.

A groan vibrated in his chest. "Don't do this to me, Mar—Victoria. Don't do this to us."

"I liked being Marla, your wife. If I could have my way, I'd never be Victoria again."

He turned, breaking her embrace. There was so much hurt, so much wanting in his eyes, it was painful to look at him. "You can't change who you are, Victoria. Neither can I. Life doesn't work that way."

"It could if you wanted it to badly enough."

With a blurring speed that was almost violent, and

certainly desperate, his arms closed around her. He
pulled her tight against his chest, covering her mouth
with his. His taste was tart with the flavor of grain
and hops, his breathing hard. His shirt stretched tautly
across his shoulders, his muscles rippling beneath her
palms.

Dear heaven, the gentle lover of last night who'd
taken her so tenderly was now ravaging her mouth.
Her body pulsated with the shock of his taking her so
roughly. She made a sound low in her throat. Acqui-
escence? Or was it pleasure? Her heart lunged wildly
at his intensity, his loss of control. Elation filled her
at the knowledge that she had the power to bring him
to this moment.

Only one last bit of light remained in the western
sky and stars began to glow, burning through the twi-
light in the same way Johnny's kisses burned through
her fears. For him, she could be Marla, a woman
made to love and be loved in return.

Dimly, she was aware he'd torn her blouse away,
buttons scattering onto the linoleum floor. Before she
returned Rita's shirt, she'd have to—

"Marla! I need..." His cry was that of a starving
man hungry with desire. Lifting her in his arms, he
carried her toward the bedroom.

"Johnny...the baby."

"She's fine. She's asleep." On her blanket, Terri
rested safely out of harm's way.

It occurred to Victoria she'd started something
there was only one way to finish. Not that she wanted
him to stop. But no man had ever literally swept her

off her feet before. She felt giddy. Breathless. Dizzy with the thrill of it. She was as far from icy and frigid as a woman could be, and the realization made her bold.

They tumbled onto the bed. He tugged off her slacks and undies. She stripped him of his shirt as he took her nipple into his mouth, the tug of his lips on her making her insides clench. She arched up to him, wanting more, needing more.

"Johnny," she gasped, imploring him to end this sweet torture.

"Yes." He undid the snap of his jeans, then the zipper.

Suddenly, he was inside her, filling her. Her body shuddered at the sweet sensation of invasion, a sensation that still felt so new and wondrous. Her hands clung to his shoulders; her legs linked around his waist even as he drove into her again. Pain and pleasure mixed in a potent combination.

"Johnny!"

"Don't ask me to stop, kitten. Please, don't ask me to stop."

"I won't." She wanted to say she'd never tell him to stop—not now, not a hundred years from now— but he'd stolen her breath away. Tension coiled through her, tightening her body until she was sure she'd explode with it. She cried out, though her sob was muffled by the taste of him.

"I don't mean to hurt you."

"You're not." No other man had brought her to such a fiery pitch. Only Johnny. *Her* Johnny. Gentle or fierce, he was her noble knight. Only if he sent her away would her pain be unbearable.

The explosion that had been building burst on her. Her scream came from low in her throat as her body convulsed around him. He thrust once more, then again and she felt his responding climax deep within her. A guttural sound ripped from his chest in a primitive sob that tore at her in ways she didn't fully understand.

The quiet afterward was like the calm following a storm. Tides ebbed and flowed. Their sweat-sheened bodies clung to each other. Somewhere outside, a sea gull cried in search of its mate or one last meal before it slept.

Victoria had been tired before, but now exhaustion slipped over her like a warm blanket. She edged toward sleep, the press of Johnny's weight still on top of her. In a minute, she'd have to retrieve Terri from the living room, put her in the bassinet, but for now she'd relish the feel of Johnny, his nearness.

"This isn't going to work, you know," he said, lifting himself away.

Chill ocean air raised gooseflesh on her body. Desperately, she tried to open her heavy-lidded eyes. "What are you talking about?"

"I don't have anything to offer you, Victoria. Nothing."

"You can't mean that." From the beginning, he'd demonstrated more giving than any man she'd ever known.

"You're a millionaire, aren't you?"

"Hmm. I suppose." Several times over, but she hadn't added up her assets lately. The figures weren't terribly important to her.

"We come from different worlds, Victoria. I've clawed my way up to being chief of police and I'm a damn good one. But the country club isn't my scene."

"I didn't even know there was a country club in del Oro."

"You know what I mean. We're not exactly a good match for each other."

Tears stung her eyes. The irony of what he was saying struck her as ludicrous. All her life, men had pursued her because of her money, or rather, her father's wealth and prestige. Only David had slipped past her defenses, convincing her that he'd only been interested in her love. Now Johnny, a man who'd shown her what real love could be, was rejecting her because she had a fat bank account. Somehow the story was the same. *She* wasn't good enough to fit into his world.

As she had already learned, life wasn't fair.

It took her a long while to go to sleep even after she'd nursed the baby in the middle of the night. When Terri's cries woke her again, Johnny was gone, the house strangely empty without him.

She carried the baby into the living room and stood for a moment by the fireplace. With her fingertip, she caressed her blue knight. Noble he might be, but he'd broken her heart. His betrayal was so unexpected, she felt blindsided.

Terri's insistent cries reminded Victoria she couldn't wallow in self-pity. She had a child to raise, a child to love. She'd once promised herself she would start over.

Now was the time to begin. A man couldn't bring her happiness. She'd have to find that on her own.

And the first step was to contact the Realtor in San Luis Obispo. Clearly, Johnny wanted her out of his house and his life as soon as possible. She had no choice but to accommodate him.

FOR THE NEXT TWO DAYS, Johnny buried himself in his work. He left the house early and stayed at the office until late. He rationalized that he'd been taking too many days off. He needed to catch up, which wasn't exactly a lie. He conferred with the city manager and mayor on budget issues and met with his department's senior staff. But mostly he couldn't deal with seeing Marla—Victoria.

God, how he missed her and the baby even though they were still living in his house. When he came home after they'd gone to bed, he could still catch a whiff of Marla's perfume and Terri's baby powder. In the bathroom, he'd fist a handful of panty hose drying on the shower rod and wish he could feel the strength of Marla's legs wrapped around him. When the baby cried in the night, he wanted to be the one to bring her to Marla, to hold them both while she nursed the baby.

But that wasn't going to happen. He had to get used to being alone again. That's the way life was.

Returning from yet another meeting with the city manager, Johnny nodded to Patty. From her place at the dispatch desk, she gestured him over.

"What's up?" he asked. So far as he knew, the town had been quiet all day. Grimly, he realized he'd half welcome a crime spree as a distraction.

"Looks like del Oro has made the big time. You've got a couple of feds waiting in your office."

His brows shot up. "FBI?"

"Postal inspectors. At least, that's what their badges said."

"That's different. Somebody in town must be running a postal scam." As police chief, he wouldn't get wind of postal violations until the authorities were ready to make an arrest in his jurisdiction. They'd probably dropped by as a courtesy.

He walked into his office to find two middle-aged men, one of them sitting in his chair with his feet propped up on Johnny's desk. The soles of his shoes were nearly worn through, and both men wore gray suits that looked slightly frayed around the edges. Definitely not the spit-and-polish image of FBI agents.

"Gentlemen. I'm Chief Fuentes. What can I do for you?"

The one inspector's feet hit the floor with a bang. "Tommy Tompkins here, and my partner, Hal Donovan. Postal Inspector's Office, San Francisco." They both produced IDs.

"Right." Johnny shook their hands and Tommy edged away from the desk. "What's up?"

"We have a mail-fraud case we've been pursuing

for a couple of months," Tompkins, the senior man, began. He had thinning hair and a sallow complexion. His partner's red hair was beginning to gray.

"We were about to make an arrest when the suspect fled the area," the redhead said.

"Took us a while to get a new lead on her whereabouts."

"Her?" Johnny questioned.

"She was an accomplice to her husband, who lost an argument with a telephone pole before we had a handle on the case. When she fled, the money was all in her accounts. We've been waiting for her to turn up so we could nail her."

An uneasy feeling skittered along the back of Johnny's neck. "Have you got a name for her?"

"Sure." Smirking, the redhead slipped his hands into his pockets. "She's a real looker, too, from what we've heard."

"We've got a federal arrest warrant right here." Tompkins patted his jacket pocket. "This may be a little awkward, Chief, but we hope you'll cooperate and won't give us a hard time. The warrant's for Victoria Stapleton."

Chapter Thirteen

A muscle flexed in Johnny's jaw. His fists clenched. "Victoria Stapleton is not a criminal. She doesn't have a dishonest bone in her body."

In the face of Johnny's barely controlled fury, Tompkins backed up a step. "We heard you might be personally involved with the suspect."

"You've got that damn straight. And I'm tellin' you, whatever you've heard, whatever case you think you've got, Mar—Victoria is innocent."

"Think again, Chief Fuentes. Mrs. Stapleton's signature is on the deposit slips. She cashed the checks of the people she and her husband defrauded. And we've got more than one victim who she personally persuaded to invest in bogus companies. Their life savings, man. Old people who couldn't afford it. This is not a nice lady you've been harboring."

"I haven't been *harboring* a criminal. She had amnesia, for God's sake!"

"Damn convenient, don't you think?" Tompkins said.

They were wrong, and Johnny was damn well going to prove it. But knowing the way the feds worked, he wouldn't be able to prevent her arrest. Not with a warrant already in hand. Damn! After all her troubles, Marla didn't deserve this.

"She's got a baby," he said. "She won't be able to leave—"

"We heard that, too. We've arranged for county social services—"

"No. I'll take care of the baby. Or my sister will—"

"Unless you're the kid's father, you've got no say. Standard procedure means we've got to—."

"Damn your procedures! No way is she going to turn her baby over to some bureaucrat to stick her in foster care. I won't have it. And whatever you may think she's done, she has some rights about who's going to take care of her baby."

"So you're saying you're the kid's father?"

"Yeah. I'm saying that." If Dr. Bernie hadn't gotten around to changing the birth certificate, Johnny's name would still be there. Let the feds challenge that!

Tompkins narrowed his eyes. Donovan kept on smirking.

"We're going to pick her up now," Tompkins announced.

Johnny blocked his way. "Give me a minute to make a phone call."

"If you warn her we're coming and she flees, you'll be abetting—"

"Ease off, Tompkins. I know the law. I'm calling

my sister to come get the baby. And I'll be the one to arrest her.''

"You've got a conflict of interest—''

"You may have a federal warrant, but this is my town, my job." And it would practically kill him to be the one to arrest Victoria.

When he applied to the police academy, they'd asked what he'd do if he caught his brother or sister committing a crime. He'd known the answer had damn well better be he'd make the arrest or he would've been bounced from the academy in an instant.

He'd never expected to be put to an even tougher test.

VICTORIA HAD MADE A LIST of everything she needed to do before she could move into her new house. About the only thing she'd accomplished so far was buying a new car, which she'd done right off the lot of the dealership in San Luis Obispo. She grinned wryly at the thought of the minivan parked in front of Johnny's house. She was well on her way to becoming a typical suburban housewife, with the minor exception that she didn't have a husband.

A lump formed in her throat as loneliness assailed her. It didn't help to dwell on what she couldn't change. Johnny had been avoiding her for the past two days, ever since they'd made love. His message was clear. He didn't want her—at least not for the long haul.

They weren't a good match.

Her eyes blurred and she checked her watch. As soon as Terri woke from her nap, they'd have to leave to meet the workmen who would be measuring for carpets and window coverings at the new house. If she had time after that, she'd stop by the college to pick up registration forms for the fall quarter.

A car pulled into the driveway and her heart stumbled. Johnny was home early. She went to the door to meet him, noticing a second vehicle arrive right after Johnny's squad car. She frowned as two men got out, spoke to Johnny, then they all headed for the front door.

She backed away. A little frantically, she glanced at the knight on the mantel, her good-luck charm. Not that it had done her much good in helping her claim a piece of Johnny's heart.

His dark eyes looked troubled as he entered. The two men, who appeared as grim as Johnny, followed him inside. She cocked her head, afraid to ask what was wrong.

"Kitten, these two men are postal inspectors." He drew an audible breath, and for a moment his gaze slid away from hers. "They're...I have to arrest you."

She looked at him stupidly. "Arrest me?"

"For mail fraud, Mrs. Stapleton," the older of the two men said.

She almost laughed. The thought of her committing any crime was ludicrous. But these men were deadly serious. "You must be mistaken. I haven't..."

A pair of handcuffs appeared and the stranger began reciting her rights in a raspy monotone.

"Johnny? What's going on?" She took another step away.

"Lose the cuffs, Tompkins," Johnny said. "I told you I'd take care of this. Victoria isn't going to resist arrest."

"Of course I am," she blurted out. "I haven't done anything wrong."

"Take it easy, kitten. Somebody's made a mistake, that's all. We'll get it straightened out. But for now, you'll have to go with these inspectors."

"I can't go anywhere! I've got a baby in the other room. She's about to wake up any minute. She'll be hungry."

"I called Rita."

"Rita can't feed her. I'm *nursing* Terri." Johnny knew that. Why would he even suggest such a thing?

"Social services will take care of everything," the second man said. "You don't have to worry, ma'am."

"Social services!" Victoria gasped.

"Rita's going to bring some formula. It'll be okay, kitten. I promise."

"Promise? Promise?" She nearly screamed the words, backing up again, this time toward the hallway, toward where Terri slept innocently in her bassinet. "You're all crazy if you think I'm going to leave my baby. I haven't *done* anything. Besides, I've got an appointment to meet the carpet man." The inanity of that statement struck her like a slap in the face. Here she was worried about measuring for carpets when she should be worried about losing her freedom. And her child.

A woman with tightly permed hair appeared at the open front door, so plump she practically filled the doorway. "Hello there, everyone. I'm Clarisa Fipp from social services. Here to pick up our little bundle." She waddled into the room.

"Forget it, lady," Johnny barked. "We've made other arrangements."

"I have my orders," she protested. Her hair jiggled when she abruptly came to a halt.

"Let's get going," the gray-haired man said, weighing the handcuffs threateningly in his palm. "It's a long drive to San Francisco."

"San Fran—"

"That's the closest federal court," Johnny explained. "They have jurisdiction."

Rita showed up at the front door. "Johnny, what's all this nonsense about Marla's being arrested?"

From the other room, Terri let out a wail.

Victoria bolted for her baby. The two postal inspectors ran after her, one of them yelling about an attempted escape. She thought that was ridiculous until she found herself face down on the floor, her hands twisted behind her back and Johnny trying to defend her.

Then she knew she was in very serious trouble. These men meant business.

VICTORIA SAT in the back seat of Inspector Tompkins's car. He and his partner were riding up front;

she and Johnny were handcuffed together.

"You really shouldn't have hit that man," she said mildly. They'd been driving for about two hours. It had taken her that long to calm down to something resembling a subdued hysteria. And now, when they spoke softly, the two men in the front couldn't hear their conversation.

"I didn't like the way he had his hands on you."

Neither had Victoria. Though at the time she'd been far more worried about that pompous social worker snatching Terri from her arms. "What's the mayor going to think about the town's police chief getting in a brawl?"

Johnny shrugged. His left eye was nearly swollen shut. The redheaded agent had a broken nose. "They'll probably file an official complaint with the town fathers, then drop the charges."

Leaning back, she rested her head on his shoulder. The adrenaline that had been pumping through her veins had slowed, leaving her feeling exhausted. "The city council ought to be thrilled with the news that the woman you've been pretending to be married to—which is odd enough—has now been arrested for mail fraud."

"We'll work it out."

"David must've been up to something I wasn't aware of."

"Which means you're an innocent bystander."

"That's not what Tompkins and his buddy seem to think."

Under his breath, he used an unpleasant epithet to describe the duo.

"They also have the key to these handcuffs." She lifted her hand and his came up, too.

"At least we got rid of that Clarisa person."

Thank heavens! she thought on a sigh. "Terri will be all right, won't she? With Rita, I mean."

"You know my sister. The baby will be fine."

"I was surprised you told everyone you're Terri's father."

"Yeah, well, that's how it feels even if it isn't true. And these two jerks…" He nodded toward the front seat. "They don't know any better."

In spite of her worries, the knowledge that Johnny had claimed Terri as his own flesh and blood warmed Victoria. Unfortunately, that same thought stimulated her breasts. She really needed to express some milk, but this was hardly the place to do it. And the more that time passed, the more uncomfortable she'd become.

"How long will I have to stay in jail?" she asked.

"At least until morning. There'll be a hearing and the magistrate will set bail."

"Johnny, I can't be away from Terri that long."

"I know, kitten. We'll get you out as soon as we can."

"How are you going to manage that when you're as likely to be locked up as I am?"

"I told Rita who to call."

"Oh."

Johnny brought her hand to his lips, kissing her palm gently. "We'll get through this, kitten."

She held that promise close to her heart a few hours later as she was booked and placed in a cell with a woman who'd robbed a bank and one who'd been caught smuggling drugs on an airplane from China. She shivered at the humiliation of being locked up with two hardened criminals.

Thank heavens her wealthy parents hadn't lived to see her brought this low. Status and appearances had meant everything to them. Once again, she'd failed them, though this time it wasn't her own doing.

Shuddering, she recalled why she hated small, dark places. She'd gotten a terrible report card when she'd been about ten and knew her parents would be deeply disappointed. So she'd sneaked into the house after school and hidden in the closet. Though she knew her parents must be frantic, she'd stayed there all night, trembling at every strange noise in the house. It seemed better to remain hidden than to face their stern disapproval.

By morning, her full bladder forced her from her hiding place. Her parents met her at the bedroom door. They'd known all along where she was. They'd let her stew in her own sense of failure.

After that, they seemed to expect even less of her.

THE FIRST PERSON SHE SAW in the courtroom the next morning was Johnny. Freshly shaved and dressed in a neatly pressed uniform, he looked wonderful until she got a close look at his swollen eye. It made her wince just to see the vivid discoloration.

"You all right, kitten?"

"I'm fine. Did a doctor take a look at that eye of yours?"

"I've had black eyes before. They pretty much take care of themselves."

She reached out to touch him. "But you should've put ice—"

The matron forcefully moved her away from Johnny and toward the defendant's table.

"What about your arrest?" she asked over her shoulder, more worried at the moment about Johnny than she was about herself.

"They've been very understanding. No charges were filed." He gestured past her. "Your attorney is Marvin Hutch from San Luis."

In search of her unknown lawyer, she glanced around the small audience of onlookers seated behind the railing. To her astonishment, Ann Drummond was there and so was her twin, Jodie, in the very front row. They both gave her a wave and a thumbs-up sign. Mama was sitting right next to them and Dora was one row back.

Their presence staggered Victoria. She'd never expected anyone from del Oro to drive all the way to San Francisco for an early morning hearing. They all had their own lives to lead. Yet they'd come to support her.

She couldn't think of a single acquaintance in Marin who would have been there for her.

All night, she'd struggled against tears of humiliation and the press of fear that tightened her chest. Now she lost the battle. In all the time she'd known these dear people, she'd never given them a thing. Along with no memory of who she was, she'd had no money. Even so, they'd willingly given her their friendship.

Turning, her knees weak, she sank onto a chair at the defendant's table. Tears rolled unchecked down her cheeks, but she didn't care. The tears were as much from joy as they were a result of her fear and humiliation.

Never in her life had she felt richer than she did at this moment. She had friends who truly cared about her. And if Johnny couldn't love her in the way she wanted him to, she could at least count him as a friend, too.

A distinguished gentleman wearing an Armani suit joined her, extending his hand.

"I'm Marvin Hutch, your attorney, Mrs. Stapleton. Johnny has advised me of your situation." He placed his leather briefcase on the table, undid the button on his jacket and took the chair next to Victoria. "This hearing will be brief. The magistrate will arraign you, I'll request that you be released on your own recognizance, and we'll have you back home in no time at all."

"I haven't done anything wrong."

Exuding confidence, he gave her a warm, encouraging smile. Not a single strand of his silver-gray hair was out of place. "I have every intention of pleading you innocent."

"I have a baby—"

"She's downstairs with Rita Diaz waiting for you. You'll have her in your arms again in no time," he told her in a voice rich with understanding.

Thank heavens! For the first time in nearly eighteen hours, Victoria breathed a little easier. She felt that she was in good hands with Marvin Hutch.

"Whatever crime has been committed," she said, "I had no part in it. David never discussed the business with me." But she should have sensed from the beginning that her husband lacked the strong ethics her adoptive father had had in such great abundance. Apparently, David had fooled him, too.

"I haven't seen the evidence as yet, but try not to be too concerned."

That was easy for the attorney to say. He hadn't spent a night in jail, breasts painfully full, with two women who shook the cell with their snores.

When the magistrate arrived, everyone in the courtroom stood. The proceedings went so quickly Victoria had some trouble following all the legalese. She did catch *grand theft mail fraud* and gasped aloud. And when Mr. Hutch asked that she be released on her own recognizance, the prosecuting attorney objected, her shrill voice having the same effect on Victoria as fingernails on a blackboard.

"The defendant has already fled the jurisdiction once, Your Honor." Looking down her hooked nose, the prosecutor sent Victoria a narrow-eyed glance. "We believe she continues to be a flight risk."

"That's nonsense," Victoria said under her breath to her attorney. "Where would I go with a month-old baby? And I hadn't meant to—"

He waved her to be quiet.

"We are requesting a million-dollar bond, Your Honor," the prosecutor concluded.

This time, everyone in the room gasped.

Mr. Hutch stood to argue on Victoria's behalf and eventually convinced the judge to lower the bond to half a million dollars.

As the matron led Victoria back to a holding cell, she began to realize just what it was like to be a criminal.

Worse, the wait to be released lengthened into the afternoon. She couldn't imagine why there was such a delay. She had plenty of money to make bail and had given Marvin Hutch a power of attorney to withdraw the necessary funds from her accounts.

At long last, a matron took her back to the room where she'd been booked. Johnny and Mr. Hutch were waiting for her.

Johnny opened his arms to her. Gratefully, she went into his embrace. She clung to him, feeling his reassuring strength. She wished she didn't need him so much, want him so much, not when he didn't feel the same way. She'd have to stand on her own two feet. But not right now.

"What took so long?" she asked, finally easing

back, though Johnny still kept one arm firmly hooked around her waist.

The attorney handed Victoria an envelope with her personal possessions, the watch and earrings she'd been wearing when she was arrested. "The government has frozen your assets, including all your bank and investment accounts, and placed liens on your property," he explained.

"Liens? Can they do that?" she asked, appalled.

"They want to make sure there are enough funds available for restitution should they gain a conviction in your case."

"And in the meantime, I'm broke? If they froze all my assets, how did they expect me to raise bail money?"

"You friends have taken care of it," Mr. Hutch said.

"My friends?" She turned to Johnny.

"Ann and Jodie," he said. "Dora. Mama, too."

She shook her head, stunned, confused. "They don't have that kind of money."

"I think Jodie took out a personal loan from the bank where she works. Ann got one from her folks. Dora and Mama had some savings."

Tears stung her eyes, and her throat ached. "And you?"

He shrugged. "I borrowed against my retirement fund. We'll all get it back when you make your court appearance."

Amazement swept over her, a tear slipping from the corner of her eye, sliding down her cheek to her trembling lips. She couldn't believe that people she'd known for such a short time would actually borrow money for her. They couldn't *know* she was innocent. Not really. After all, her amnesia would have been darn convenient if she'd been fleeing arrest.

She thought about her friends in Marin County, those with whom she'd served on committees to raise funds for charitable organizations, and wondered if any of them would have helped her if she'd needed them. Oh, they'd been kind to her face when David died, but behind her back she'd caught them snickering about his lover. No one had offered her the true friendship the people of del Oro seemed to give so easily.

"Thank you, Johnny," she whispered. "Tell the others—"

He pressed a finger to her lips, gently wiped a wayward tear from her cheek with his thumb. "Let's get Terri and go home, kitten. You can tell them yourself."

Chapter Fourteen

"That isn't my signature."

"The postal authorities believe it is."

Victoria shook her head at the papers Marvin Hutch had slid across his desk to her. They named Victoria Stapleton as vice president and financial secretary of Investments Unlimited, Inc., one of several fraudulent companies David had created to sell stock in nonexistent firms to unwary investors.

It had been a week since Victoria's arrest. Only now was she seeing the evidence against her. Taken at face value, it was damning.

"I've never seen these forms before and I never knowingly signed them."

"Knowingly?" Johnny questioned. He was sitting in the chair next to her, and they both faced Marvin across his mahogany desk. The corner office had a hundred-and-eighty-degree view of San Luis Obispo and the surrounding hills with burgeoning residential areas marching up them.

"Sometimes David would have me sign papers, like our joint tax returns. He was always in a rush and said not to bother my pretty little head with the details. Like a fool, I didn't always read them.''

She shuddered at her stupidity. He'd taken advantage of her in every way. Violated her while subtly undermining her already shaky self-confidence. Having discovered how he'd swindled thousands of innocent investors, she hated him more now than when she'd learned of his adultery.

''I was so blind to what he was doing,'' she admitted.

Johnny covered her hand with his. ''He was a born con artist. There was no way you could've known that. Look at how many others he fooled.''

Small consolation for either her or David's other victims, she thought as she studied the contrast between Johnny's hand and hers. His complexion was shades darker than hers, his fingers square and not at all aristocratic as David's had been. Yet Johnny had more integrity in his little finger than David had had in his entire body.

She desperately wished she could feel Johnny's hands caressing her again, but he'd continued to avoid any intimate contact between them.

He was solicitous of her. Encouraging. Supportive. All the things a friend should be. But he wasn't her husband. And he didn't love her.

The frustration was getting to her. She couldn't stay much longer in his house. If nothing else, she was likely to attack him one of these nights when she simply couldn't stand not being in his arms for another moment.

Marvin leaned back in his chair, making the springs creak, and tented his fingertips together beneath his chin. "We'll call in a handwriting expert and someone to do a computer analysis of the signatures. It's simple enough to forge a signature these days."

"How long will that take?" she asked.

"It's hard to tell. Perhaps a week or more."

Impatience with the justice system—and a bad case of unrequited love—drove her to her feet. "Mr. Hutch, isn't there some way that the authorities will let me take my furniture out of storage so I can live in my house? I'm not going anywhere. I just can't keep on this way." Living with a man she loved who couldn't love her back.

"There's no hurry for you to move out of my place," Johnny said.

She glared at him. "Yes, there is."

"I'll see what I can do," Marvin said. "The lien will remain on the house until this matter is resolved, but I see no legal impediment to your occupancy."

"It'd be nice if they released enough money for me to live on, too."

"That would seem a reasonable request."

Then why hadn't he made the request on her behalf a week ago? She smiled sweetly. "I'd appreciate whatever you can do to expedite matters, Mr. Hutch."

"Of course, Mrs. Stapleton." He rose. "You might wish to take along copies of the affidavits from victims of this investment fraud. The amount of money involved is quite astounding. Little wonder the federal authorities are looking for restitution wherever they can find it.''

She accepted a file folder that was a good two inches thick. ''After David died and the dust had settled, I found there wasn't much more in our accounts than there had been when I inherited from my parents. I don't think my money came from the victims.''

''Yes, well, there may be offshore accounts. Those will be difficult to trace. Meanwhile, the bank records suggest the illegal funds were laundered through several of your local accounts.''

''David was really slick,'' she said with as much disgust for her own foolishness as for David's criminal behavior. ''He and his girlfriend had probably been planning to run off after they amassed enough money in Grenada or somewhere. They just waited a little too long and met a telephone pole head-on first. There were airline tickets in David's pocket the night he died. He traveled so frequently, until now—until this thing came up—I didn't make the connection.''

The bile of betrayal rose in her throat. ''He'd been planning to leave the country with that woman, and leave me pregnant and on my own to face the authorities when they caught on to the scam. He framed me, dammit!''

She spilled out her revelation in a rush. Marvin nodded sagely. Johnny swore succinctly.

A half hour later, after reviewing more of the so-called evidence against her, she and Johnny left the attorney's office. When they reached the parking lot, Johnny opened the car door for her.

"You know you can stay as long as you want at my place," he said. "I think Marvin is going to get this whole mess straightened out in a hurry, now that we figured out what happened."

"I have to go, Johnny. I have to make a life for myself and Terri."

He hated that sad look in her eyes that made the green turn all misty, hated even more the gut-twisting realization that she really meant it this time. When she was arrested, he'd been given a reprieve, albeit a short one, to keep her with him. Now his time was up.

"I'll miss you. Both of you." His throat felt as though he'd swallowed sandpaper.

"You can come visit whenever you like. You know where I'll be."

"Sure." But a clean cut healed faster than one where the scab kept coming off. "I wouldn't want little Terri to forget me."

"She won't. Ever." Turning, Victoria—his Marla—got into the passenger seat.

Johnny walked slowly around the back of the car, trying to pull himself together, knowing she was right to go. He ran a hand through his hair in frustration. His life would return to normal, to the way it had been before he found her walking all alone on the beach—his own personal sea nymph.

Damn! He hadn't realized how much love could hurt.

The next day, Marvin called with the news Victoria could move into her house whenever she was ready.

She left two days later, taking Terri and Beau with her.

Damn if he didn't miss the dog, too.

MAMA STORMED INTO Johnny's office. Mama *never* came to his office. She wouldn't want to interrupt his important work—work that he hadn't been able to get done for the past week since Marla left him. All that time, he hadn't been eating, hadn't been sleeping—

He was on his feet in an instant. "What's wrong?" He had visions of his nephews or niece crushed under a car, or one of his sisters lying comatose in the hospital.

"You, that's what's wrong. I raised an idiot, that's what. How am I gonna explain to your papa when I see him—God rest his soul—that our Juan is loco, eh? How am I gonna do that, will you tell me?"

He shoved the door closed behind her. "What are you talking about?"

"That girl, what else? Our Marla. You sent her away, and her with a tiny baby to take care of."

Now he understood. Sort of. "Her name's Victoria."

"She was your wife. You can't just throw her out like she was week-old trash. You had an obligation."

"Mama, we weren't married. It was all pretend." Although what he felt for her seemed pretty damn real.

"Bah. I saw how you looked at each other. It doesn't matter the priest hadn't said the words over you yet. She loved you."

Forcefully, he made his mother sit down. "She *needed* me, Mama. She didn't have anyone else. That's not the same as love."

"You think your mama doesn't know the difference between love and need? I'm not that old, Juanito. I remember. And in case nobody told you, they go together. If she loves you, of course she needs you. And the same goes for you. *You* need her."

He didn't want to admit that. "We weren't right for each other."

"What? She's a girl. You're a boy." She gestured wildly. "What's not right about that?"

"Don't you understand? She's too good for me."

Mama stared at him blankly. "She's gonna be a nun? How's she gonna do that with a baby?"

"No, no. I mean..." He walked to the window. From this vantage point, he could see the main street of Mar del Oro and the slowly moving traffic. "You should have seen her house in Marin, Mama. It was huge, with a four-car garage, acres of lawn. A big circular driveway that could've parked ten cars, maybe more. No way would I ever be able to give her anything like that."

"Maybe that's not what she wants, *mi hijo,* my son," she said softly. She'd followed him across the room and now she palmed his cheek as if he were a little boy again. Her dark eyes, so like his own, were filled with love. But she didn't understand.

"The house she bought in San Luis Obispo is three, maybe four times as big as my place. She paid cash."

"A woman cannot curl up with a house. Your papa

and I had nothing, yet we had everything we needed. This Marla of yours—or Victoria, if that's what she wants to be called—is a good woman. I cannot believe she would rather sleep alone in a big house instead of lying next to you even if all you had was a single blanket to cover her with.''

A part of Johnny wanted to believe that. But it didn't seem fair to Victoria to offer her so little, comparatively speaking, when she'd had a lifetime of wealth.

Sure, he had a house overlooking the beach, prime real estate with a steep mortgage to go with it, plus another chunk of change going to help Mama make ends meet. The salary of a small-town police chief didn't cover extras like shopping trips to London or buying a top-of-the-line Mercedes off the showroom floor. That's what Victoria was used to.

Whatever love she felt for him was too likely to wither in the face of reality, like a grape crop shrivels and turns bitter when it doesn't get enough rain.

He didn't want to put either one of them through that misery.

VICTORIA SET THE PILE of affidavits aside, leaned her head back on the couch and looked up at the high cathedral ceiling in her new living room. Reading how David had stolen the life savings of so many elderly people had brought tears to her eyes. How could he have been so cruel? So selfish?

This had been her first chance to sit for a few minutes since she'd moved into the house a week ago, and she'd taken the opportunity to go through the file while Terri was napping. She felt so heartsick over the lives her husband had ruined that she was almost sorry she'd taken the time to read the victims' stories.

Perhaps the authorities would be able to locate the money in offshore accounts, though Marvin Hutch didn't hold out much hope for that. And the prosecutor was still determined to see Victoria behind bars.

The doorbell rang, startling her. After spending most of the day unpacking cardboard cartons and washing crystal stemware, she was hardly presentable for company.

She looked through the peephole, and her heart gave a little lurch. "Mama?" she said, opening the door in surprise.

In a critical assessment, Dolores Fuentes looked her up and down. "You look like hell." Stepping into the entryway, she took Victoria in her arms, hugging her against her full bosom.

It was all Victoria could do not to burst into tears. That Mama Fuentes could be so loving astounded her. She'd never before experienced such unconditional acceptance as she had in del Oro.

"This is a nice house," Mama said, releasing Victoria from her embrace and giving her cheek a little pat. "Big for just you and your little *bebé,* my Terri."

"I do have some extra rooms," she conceded. "One of them I'm going to turn into an art studio for myself. I'm going to try a little painting on my own. And Terri will have a playroom."

"That's nice for a little girl. But she's gonna be lonely without little brothers and sisters."

"She'll have friends." Victoria would see to that. Ann and Jodie had helped her move in, and Dora had already dropped by once. Victoria would make sure that her daughter learned how to develop friendships like that, too. Giving her child brothers and sisters didn't look like a viable option any time soon, particularly since she couldn't imagine anyone except Johnny as their father.

Dolores walked around the living room, examining but not touching Victoria's display of small sculptures that rested on French provincial end tables. "Friends are not the same as family."

"Mama—"

"My son says he's not good enough for you."

She gasped. "That's not true."

"He thinks you need this big house and all this fanciness to make you happy."

"No." She'd never given her wealth much thought until Johnny had made an issue of it. She only knew that others had *used* her because of her money, her late husband included.

"Then you must tell him he's wrong."

"Mama, it wouldn't do any good. He doesn't love me."

"Why do you think that? He's losing weight. He doesn't look like he's sleeping good. To me, that adds up to a man in love."

"If he loved me, he would've asked me to stay with him—as his wife, not just as a roommate."

"But my son is not very bright, *sí?* He gets an idea into that thick skull of his and he won't let it go. He was the same way playing football. He'd put his head down and run right at those boys who weighed three hundred pounds. They almost killed him. But would he quit? Not my Juan. He always thought he could do it on his own." She lifted her arms in a gesture of frustration. "What he gets in his head he keeps there until somebody knocks it out of him."

"I hardly think I can hire an entire football team to beat him up." Though it was a thought worth considering. No other inspiration had come to her.

"You're a smart girl. You'll think of something."

Mama apparently gave Victoria more credit for intelligence than she deserved.

From the built-in intercom came the sound of Terri waking and letting the world know she didn't like to be alone.

"Would you like to come upstairs while I get the baby?" Victoria asked.

"*Sí.* Teresa's one of my grandbabies whether you and Johnny say so or not."

Laughing warmly, Victoria hooked her arm through Mama's. "I wouldn't have it any other way and neither would Terri."

Later that evening, after she'd put Terri down for the night, Victoria paced the house alone. What she had once hoped would be a new beginning for her and her baby now felt meaningless. Four walls and a roof, no matter how large, did not make for a home without the infusion of a great deal of love. She knew she could pour her heart and soul into this house and into raising her baby, but it would never feel complete unless Johnny was a part of the picture.

Sighing, she looked out at the lights of San Luis Obispo. It was a lovely town, really. Vibrant. Growing rapidly. Becoming more sophisticated every year with a fine cultural climate.

But it wasn't Mar del Oro.

It wasn't Johnny's town.

She glanced across the room at the file of affidavits. What irony that all those people had lost their life savings when the money had meant so much to them. Meanwhile, Victoria had more wealth than she could ever spend—assuming she was found innocent of the mail-fraud charges—and the money was the biggest obstacle keeping her from the man she loved.

She frowned, crossing the room to stare down at the files. The answer, she realized, was so obvious she wondered why she hadn't thought of it before.

She couldn't just *tell* Johnny the money wasn't important. She had to *show* him. In fact, she had to risk everything to prove to Johnny that she truly wanted to start over, that his love was all she'd ever want or need.

But working out the details and escaping federal prosecution was going to take a little time. However anxious she might be to get on with her life, for now she'd have to be patient.

JOHNNY HATED TO GO HOME to an empty house. For nearly a month, the ghosts in the place had been driving him crazy. Every time he turned around, he saw Marla. At the sink humming tunelessly as she washed the dishes. Or sitting at the table painting Dora's miniatures. Or in his bed, waiting for him.

He'd hear Terri crying in the night.

Or hear the silly mutt yapping at the waves down below on the beach.

He was thinking about selling the place.

Entering the diner in town, he headed toward the back booth only to discover a couple of tourists were sitting there. He had to settle for a booth closer to the front.

The waitress brought him a menu. Nora, he thought her name was, or maybe Noreen. He couldn't remember. Tina had moved out of town a couple of weeks ago. This one was younger, maybe eighteen or nineteen, hardly old enough to be out of high school.

"Just a bowl of minestrone," he said, waving off the menu. If he didn't get back his appetite soon, he'd have to punch a new hole in his belt. "And coffee, black."

"Yes, sir."

Damn, he felt old.

The girl had just brought him a mug full of coffee when his pager vibrated at his waist. He checked the number. Patty wanted him.

He downed a gulp of coffee and headed for the phone behind the counter. Nora—or Noreen—didn't bat an eye.

"What's up, Patty?"

"I got a call from a woman."

"Happens all the time. Half the population are women."

"This one was acting...troubled."

He rubbed his hand along the back of his neck. He needed a haircut. "Can't someone else take the call? Where's Stu?"

"He's tied up investigating a call at the Best Western on the beach. A man reported someone stole his watch and his money clip while he was in the shower."

"Probably the woman he brought with him to the motel," he muttered. "Okay, where do I find this *troubled* woman?"

Patty gave him an address down toward the beach, not far from the center of town.

"Has she got a name?"

"She, uh, seemed a little confused about that."

"Great." *Troubled* as in mentally ill? Every town had its share.

His heart stumbled painfully as he recalled the last time he'd been called out to check on a confused woman who was walking alone on the beach. Dammit, he wanted Marla back! So what if she was as rich as Bill Gates? That meant she could buy her own Mercedes and go shopping anyplace in the world she wanted.

All he had to do was swallow his pride. That was a helluva big mouthful, he realized. A lot like eating crow. But if he didn't make the effort, if he didn't beg her to come back to him, *marry* him, he'd be lost in the morass of loneliness for the rest of his life.

Dropping a five-dollar bill on the table beside the bowl of soup, he went out to his car. He hadn't been very hungry anyway.

The address he'd been given was a small house in a row of thirty-year-old cottages that were used mostly for summer homes, the yards more sand than grass, the paint chipped. Though the porch light was on and the house well lit, he approached cautiously. Cops learned to do that.

From the back of the house, a dog came racing toward him, little more than a puppy, with short hair, floppy black ears and feet too big for his body. His tail was wagging so fast, it looked like it might fly off. If the dog wasn't Beau, he sure as hell could pass for his twin brother.

The dog leaped up to his chest.

The front door opened. "Beau! How'd you get out of the backyard?"

Johnny stood there dumbstruck as the dog raced circles around him. His mouth turned as dry as dust. For a moment, he thought he was hallucinating. "Marla?"

Backlit in the doorway, she grew very still. She was wearing a knit top and a skirt that reached her calves, almost see-through, and the hint of her silhouette showed through the material—long, well-shaped legs and hips made for making babies.

"Hello, Johnny."

He swallowed hard. "Did you call 911?"

"Actually, no. I called Patty on the office line. I didn't know if you'd think this was an emergency."

"Is it?"

"For me it is." She stepped back into the house and held the door open for him.

Beau raced up the steps. Johnny moved much slower. Patty, it dawned on him, had been doing a little matchmaking, sending him here under false pretenses.

For a few minutes, the distraction of getting Beau secured in the backyard again prevented much conversation. But when they went inside, the air was electric with awkwardness.

Johnny shoved his hands into his pockets to prevent himself from grabbing Marla and taking her right there on the worn and faded carpet.

"So how's Terri?" he asked, an unexpected rasp in his throat.

"She's fine. Sleeping. I think she misses you."

"Yeah. I miss her, too." Almost as much as he missed Marla. Together, he missed them so much it was like having his heart cut out.

"You could have come to see her."

"I know." His gaze slid away from her to check out the room. With the exception of some nice furniture and a few knickknacks, including the miniature medieval knight he'd given her, "dingy" was a good description of the place. Nothing like her house in Marin—or even the new one in San Luis Obispo. "What are you doing here?"

"This is where I live now. I'm renting month to month."

His brows shot up. "Renting? You've got a house in San Luis—"

"I sold it. Or rather, the U.S. attorney's office is taking care of that for me."

"They confiscated your property? Dammit, I thought Hutch—"

"I gave it to them. Everything I had—all my assets except my car and a small bank account—I've signed over to the attorneys who represent David's victims. Marvin worked out a deal for me with the federal prosecutor."

"She was a witch."

"She was doing her job. More importantly, David hurt a lot of people. I wanted to make it right again."

"But you didn't do anything wrong. If you went to trial, Hutch could have built a strong defense. We already proved those signatures were forgeries. You were totally innocent of any wrongdoing. You weren't the one who hurt those people. Why would you turn over all of your assets?"

She took a step forward. "I did it for you, Johnny. For you and me and Terri, who'd very much like to have you as her father."

He felt as if a steel fist had smashed into his solar plexus. If he finally understood his pride was as big as a house, he now recognized her courage was enormous. "For me?"

She edged closer. "If you still can't love me, I'll try very hard to understand. But I intend to build a life for myself and my daughter here in del Oro. I may not have any money to speak of, but I am gainfully employed. Dora's hired me to work weekends at the store and I'll still be painting miniatures for her. I've got some ideas about designing new characters, children's characters that I could sculpt myself and sell in her store as well as other galleries. In time, I should be able to make a decent living.''

''Nothing like you had before.''

''What I had before, Johnny, was a loveless marriage. Even as a child, I was starved for love without knowing what I was missing. Until I met you.''

He closed his eyes. This was a dream. Any minute now, he'd wake up. ''All that money…''

''Don't you understand? It never mattered to me. It was never *mine*. The money belonged to my parents—or to my husband. But never to *me*.'' She was standing close to him now. Close enough that he caught her fresh floral scent. ''Besides wanting to get a degree at the university, there was another reason I chose to move to San Luis Obispo.''

Hesitantly, he touched her face with his fingertips, half-afraid she'd vanish in the mist the way she did in the dreams he had of her every night. ''Why?''

''San Luis Obispo was listed as my place of birth on my birth certificate. I had this crazy idea I might, I don't know…stumble across my biological mother. We'd recognize each other instantly. There'd be this grand reunion. She'd cry. I'd cry. And magically, we'd become a family. But I know the chances of that are poor to zero.''

''Probably.'' Unable to help himself, he ran his thumb across her lower lip. Soft. Delectable. And he remembered so clearly her flavor. He ached to taste her again.

"Now I know that if I could be your wife, you and Mama, Rita and her kids and your other sisters would be all the family I'd ever need. I love you, Johnny." Tears shone in her eyes. "I don't know how else to convince you except to say that. I'm not rich. I came into this world with nothing and that pretty much is all I've got left. Please tell me it's enough."

A band tightened around his chest; the lump in his throat made it impossible to speak. *Enough?* She was more than enough to last him a lifetime.

He claimed her mouth in a fierce kiss, a kiss he intended to speak for him with all the passion, all the love, he felt inside. She melted against him, opened to him. He took everything she gave him, and he was going to ask for more. Just as soon as he could catch his breath.

He wasn't sure how long they stood there kissing before he came up for air. "I've got just one question before we find the bedroom."

She grinned at him. "I take it I've made my point."

"Absolutely. I love you and I'm going to marry you and be Terri's daddy. And at this point, I damn well wouldn't take no for an answer. But what do I call you?"

She looked at him blankly for an instant, then her smile turned coy. "Besides kitten?"

"Yeah," he laughed. "Besides that."

Framing his face between her palms, she kissed

him again. Tenderly. Seductively. "The happiest time in my life was when I was Marla. Do you suppose we could officially change my name to that? Mrs. Marla Fuentes?"

"Consider it done." He scooped her up into his arms. "Now, kitten, tell me where the bedroom is."

If you enjoyed what you just read,
then we've got an offer you can't resist!

Take 2 bestselling love stories FREE!

Plus get a FREE surprise gift!

Clip this page and mail it to Harlequin Reader Service®

IN U.S.A.	IN CANADA
3010 Walden Ave.	P.O. Box 609
P.O. Box 1867	Fort Erie, Ontario
Buffalo, N.Y. 14240-1867	L2A 5X3

YES! Please send me 2 free Harlequin American Romance® novels and my free surprise gift. Then send me 4 brand-new novels every month, which I will receive months before they're available in stores. In the U.S.A., bill me at the bargain price of $3.34 plus 25¢ delivery per book and applicable sales tax, if any*. In Canada, bill me at the bargain price of $3.71 plus 25¢ delivery per book and applicable taxes**. That's the complete price and a savings of over 10% off the cover prices—what a great deal! I understand that accepting the 2 free books and gift places me under no obligation ever to buy any books. I can always return a shipment and cancel at any time. Even if I never buy another book from Harlequin, the 2 free books and gift are mine to keep forever. So why not take us up on our invitation. You'll be glad you did!

154 HEN CNEX
354 HEN CNEY

Name	(PLEASE PRINT)	
Address	Apt.#	
City	State/Prov.	Zip/Postal Code

* Terms and prices subject to change without notice. Sales tax applicable in N.Y.
** Canadian residents will be charged applicable provincial taxes and GST.
  All orders subject to approval. Offer limited to one per household.
  ® are registered trademarks of Harlequin Enterprises Limited.

AMER99   ©1998 Harlequin Enterprises Limited

HARLEQUIN®
Makes any time special ™

WIN A DREAM

In celebration of Harlequin®'s golden anniversary

Enter to win a *dream!* You could win:

- A luxurious trip for two to
  The Renaissance Cottonwoods Resort
  in Scottsdale, Arizona, or

- A bouquet of flowers once a week for a year
  from **FTD**, or

- A $500 shopping spree, or

- A fabulous bath & body gift basket, including
  K-tel's *Candlelight and Romance* 5-CD set.

Look for **WIN A DREAM** flash on
specially marked Harlequin® titles by
Penny Jordan, Dallas Schulze,
Anne Stuart and Kristine Rolofson
in October 1999*.

FTD

RENAISSANCE.
COTTONWOODS RESORT
SCOTTSDALE, ARIZONA

K·TEL

"Fascinating—you'll want to take
this home!"
—**Marie Ferrarella**

"Each page is filled with a brand-new
surprise."
—**Suzanne Brockmann**

"Makes reading a new and joyous
experience all over again."
—**Tara Taylor Quinn**

See what all your favorite authors
are talking about.

Coming October 1999 to a retail store near you.

HARLEQUIN®
Makes any time special ™

Silhouette®